Finch Books by Isabelle Drake:

Cherry Grove
Best Friends Never

Cherry Grove

BEST FRIENDS NEVER

ISABELLE DRAKE

Best Friends Never
ISBN # 978-1-78651-950-4
©Copyright Isabelle Drake 2016
Cover Art by Posh Gosh ©Copyright March 2016
Interior text design by Claire Siemaszkiewicz
Finch Books

Published in 2016 by Finch Books Newland House, The Point, Weaver Road, Lincoln, LN6 3QN, United Kingdom.

Finch Books is an imprint of Totally Entwined Group Limited.

BEST FRIENDS
NEVER

Dedication

For Walter Anthony Lucken IV
Thank you for rescuing me, on more than one
occasion, from crying into my Diet Coke alone.

Chapter One

It Doesn't Matter How You Play the Game, Only
Whether You Win or Lose

Blood red.

And death black.

Whoever picked out Cherry Grove High's school
colors was an idiot.

Either that or a serial killer.

The hideous color combination blurred across the
gym floor, spinning in the cheerleaders' skirts,
bouncing in the pom squad pom-poms and slicing
through the air in the quivering band banners. Except
for the bizarre Goth meets *Glee* effect, the scene was
flawless. Even the shouts echoing off the walls were
just right.

Outside, beyond the gleaming floor-to-ceiling
windows and careful flowerbeds, past the student
parking lot dotted with Nissans, Volvos and European
SUVs, early autumn trees shaded the tidy streets with
the first brush of rust, orange and red leaves. It was
Cherry Grove after all—anything less than perfection
would be inconceivable.

The bleachers were jammed with students, some actually excited about the annual back-to-school pep assembly, the rest just screaming like mad, glad for the chance to be crazy on the first Friday afternoon of the new school year.

From her spot at the boosters table, Lexi Welks could see it all. The teachers huddled in the corner by the wrestling mats drinking Diet Pepsis and eating popcorn, the basketball players lined up under the net, shoving each other, wanting to be the one standing closest to the podium, and the mini-mob of freshmen trying to squeeze themselves into the tiny niche that led to the empty space behind the bleachers. Apart from the chaos stood the football team, arms folded over their Cherry Grove jerseys and looking like they'd rather be anywhere but where they were — right in the center of the attention.

"Here's your baseball fundraiser auction sign-up sheet."

Monica Sanders, coming up out of nowhere like a giant weed that not even the deadliest dose of Roundup could get rid of. One of the wicked plants from *Little Shop of Horrors*.

Only this plant had a nonstop figure wrapped up in a come-screw-me black turtleneck. Half the guys in the school wanted a piece of her. The rest wanted her ACT scores.

Lexi?

Up until a week ago, she and Monica had been friends. And now Lexi was paying the price for what had seemed like fun at the time.

Monica looked over Lexi's shoulder, waved at basketball center Eric Watson, then came back with a careful smile, showing off her bleached teeth as she slid into an empty chair. "Not that the sign-up is going to do *you* any good. You know, with next year."

Lexi took the sheet, dropping it onto the table as though she wasn't the least bit concerned. Which, of course, was a huge lie. Because getting the right names on that single sheet of paper would change her whole life.

"Can I have your attention? Students?" Dr. Guerra, the superintendent, tapped on the microphone, sending out a series of heart-thumping thuds.

It worked—even the cheerleaders shut up, dropping to the floor to sit cross-legged like a row of overgrown preschoolers. "We need a moment before we get started with the pep assembly. Could everyone please welcome Officer Davenport from the Cherry Grove Police Station?"

"Where else would he be from?" one of the newspaper nerds muttered. "7-Eleven?"

The cop slid behind the mic, adjusting his navy blue uniform tie while he waited for the losers in the back rows to catch on to the idea that he had something other than the D.A.R.E. essay winners to announce. Once the room fell silent, he started talking about Jon Eagle, the kid who'd gone missing a couple of days before. Each word out of his mouth made the knots in Lexi's stomach pull tighter as images of that night skittered through her mind.

"We've been checking leads and retracing Jon's steps. We're in constant contact with his family—they'll be informed as we uncover substantial information." He flattened his square palm across his jacket lapel, pausing dramatically as he looked out at the faces. "We know how distressing this is for you all, for all of us. For those of you who'd like someone to talk with, your lead counselor, Mrs. Howell, has added appointments before and after school. She's assured me and all your parents that she'll do anything she can to help you through this difficult time."

Monica took out her pretty pink leather-bound planner and wrote down the officer's name. Then she waited, pen poised, for anything else noteworthy.

"Please keep in mind," he continued, "that we have no evidence of foul play at this time. There is no reason to believe that anyone else is in danger." He went on to add that the detective in charge thought that Jon had been in touch with kids who, for some reason, were choosing not to tell anyone. "If that's the case, we urge you to come forward at this time." Contact information flashed from the huge ceiling-mounted projector onto the wall behind the podium. Lexi barely held in her roll of nausea as Monica jotted down the counselor hours, the hotline phone number and email address with one hand, all the while texting with her other.

But that was Monica Sanders. Smart. Capable. Efficient. And a real self-serving jerk. Too bad it had taken Lexi three months to figure it out.

"Thank you for your attention." Dr. Guerra was back at the mic, struggling to say something press and parent friendly. "If we all work together, we might... Maybe we'll... Jon might..." Thank God she finally gave up, because while two band geeks in the front row were snapping pics, some of the yearbook girls over by the art teacher were starting to cry. A cloud of awkward silence filled the gym, everyone's face tense. Everyone's except Monica's. She was dumping her stuff back into her bag and getting to her feet, all while looking as fresh and fantastic as ever.

"Taylor told me to ask you if you had questions about the sign-up," she said as she pushed the chair back.

This time she wasn't even bothering to hold on to that flawless, fake smile.

"You mean like why are you even bothering with yours?" Lexi tapped her own sheet with her finger. "Because all the names that matter are going right here."

Monica practically snorted as she spun on her heels, swinging away without a reply.

Lexi watched the girl's model-perfect ass until she ducked through the red and black cluster of drumline kids clogging the double doors at the end of the gym.

Once she was sure the girl was gone for good she picked up the sheet, staring at the empty rows and imagining the names she needed scrawled across those blank lines. Planning how she'd get them there. And fighting back the fear of what Monica would do when she did.

* * * *

Something about Ash Carpenter set him apart from the other guys at Cherry Grove. Every last one of them stressed about each mundane detail of their self-absorbed lives, going through entire tubes of Clearasil picking between Vans or Etnies, Samsung or iPhone, but Ash had everything under control. Strategic. Even doing something as dull as walking across his kitchen, he looked like he could handle anything. And the fitted black T-shirt he was wearing made the watching that much better. Sure, he looked good in those tight baseball uniform pants, but the snug T-shirt showed off his hard-looking biceps and shoulders.

The lemon glow from inside the stainless steel fridge blinked as he ducked down to pull out a carton of chocolate milk. After several gulps, he leaned on the shiny silver door, slanting a sexy, boyish grin at Lexi. "You don't care about me asking you over last minute, right? It's hard to talk at school, and everything was so crazy after the pep assembly, ya know? I think that cop stressed everyone out so badly, they just rushed for the doors once it was over. I know I was glad to get out of there, get away from all the drama." He lifted his eyebrows. "As soon as I got in my car I thought of you. That's when I sent the text."

The out-of-nowhere invite had made her curious, but considering the circumstances — and the auction sign-up sheet tucked in her bag — she wasn't about to waste time with questions. "No worries about it being last minute." She flashed him her best video girl smile. "I'm just glad you did."

Stretching forward, letting her red, rescued-from-the-clearance-rack Ralph Lauren sweater pull tight across her 34Bs, she rested her elbows on the huge oak table. "Will your mom be home soon?"

Still holding the carton, Ash shoved the fridge door shut, stepped over to toss his long leg across one of the round-backed oak chairs, and sat.

"Don't know." He took another drink, wiping his full lips with his knuckles after he swallowed. "I don't have to tell her where I'll be or what I'm doing. She knows I can handle myself."

Lexi's gaze locked with his and a wave of uncertainty washed over her. What went on behind those long-lashed green eyes? Most of the time he was pretty much the typical jock — friendly but not all that open, smart but not so smart people thought he was weird. Was there more to him than he let on?

One thing was for sure — he'd come a long way since his World of Warcraft middle school days. Even went so far as to change all his friends. Now everyone at school talked about what an awesome guy he was, but the chatter was always vague. Like the new group he hung with never got inside his head.

What that meant to Lexi was that she had nothing to go on, no tidbits of useful gossip to guide her, help her pinpoint the best way to get what she needed from him—a simple signature on a sheet of paper. She looked around the kitchen, but there was nothing hanging on the fridge or sitting on the counter that revealed a private side of Ash. Nothing, until she spotted a stuffed squirrel perched on top of the corner cabinet, its beady glass eyes staring down at them. Creepy. But it was the only thing she had, so she pointed up. "Cute taxidermy. You make that in science club with your dad?"

Ash didn't turn to look where she was pointing. "Nope. My dad's favorite student did."

Lexi tried a giggle. "You had to be his favorite."

"No, I wasn't," Ash replied, his voice flat, his expression unchanging. "Never once in all the years he was in charge of the science club did he ever say I was his favorite." Ash shifted to look up at the squirrel, staring at it for a while before speaking again. "The science club building has been closed up ever since my dad died. Not even the favorite student gets to play mad scientist anymore."

The truth sat between them—now that Ash's dad was dead, he'd never get the chance to be the favorite. She scrambled for something to say, anything to keep Ash from bringing up the fact that her dad had died, too. Even though it was something they had in common, it wasn't a conversation she wanted to have. Not then. Not ever. "Parents. Whatever."

Ash's gaze inched across her shoulders, the tension gone as one corner of his mouth lifted, revealing a dimple on his left cheek. "I bet your mom doesn't understand you, not at all. I know what that's like," he went on, letting his gaze drop to the deep V of her sweater. "For people not to get you. But my mom is cool."

Glad to have the topic of dead dads behind them, Lexi shook off the sadness that always came on the heels of thoughts of her dad as she smirked and rolled her eyes. "'Mine's got her own ideas about the way things are."

And she could stay tuned to that imaginary station as long as she liked, but not Lexi. Reality wasn't a problem for her. She had a plan. College was her ticket out of Cherry Grove. After she graduated from high school she'd get out of the place and be on to an actual life that meant something.

Thinking about all the mess with Monica, that last day in Cherry Grove couldn't come fast enough. To make that happen, she had to keep up the I've-got-it-all-going-on act. The one she was in the middle of now.

"What about your stepdad?" Ash took another drink, studying her with curious eyes. "Does he understand you?"

The idea of Dale understanding anything at all almost made her laugh out loud. But that was another topic of conversation she wanted to avoid. Keeping the disgust off her face, she replied, "He got another out-of-town welding job, so he's not around."

Thank God. Even though her mom clung to the ridiculous hope that the three of them might be a family again someday, Lexi was glad Dale was trying out for Absentee Dad of the Year.

"Coach Filpot was asking about him the other day."

"Dale?" Trying to wipe the very un-cute shock off her face, she added, "Why?"

Ash set down the milk, picked up his keys, started tossing them fist to fist. The light jingle created a soft rhythm. "Since Jon graduated last year, we don't have him catching anymore."

"So?"

"It's gonna be a tough season, that's all." He started tossing the keys more quickly and the sound got louder. "Remember freshman year, when your stepdad assisted? He's good. Knows how to make people do what he wants them to. Coach wants him back."

As if she could forget Dale hanging around every minute of every practice. He'd only offered to help because at the time she'd been going out with the first baseman and being the assistant coach had given him the perfect opportunity to butt into her business. Unfortunately for her, he knew some stuff about baseball and had actually contributed to the success of the team.

"What about Jon?" Lexi asked, doing everything she could to keep the tension out of her voice. "You heard anything from him?"

Ash stopped tossing the keys. "Nope."

"He's freaked everyone out by running off like that. Just completely vanishing, without saying anything to anyone." Anxiety made her ramble on. "That's not really like him. Even though he's kind of a nerd, he's not a loner. Did somebody go with him, do you think?"

Smirking, Ash said, "Like he met someone while playing League of Legends?"

Jon the uber techy gamer. It was possible. Lexi hoped that was the case. It was way better than some of the alternatives she'd dreamed up. She reached up and swiped away the fine sheen of sweat on her forehead.

Ash tipped back in his chair. "His mom's lost it." He nodded to his cell sitting in the middle of the table. "She keeps calling me — and everybody else on the team — asking if he's called or texted. Or been on Facebook." Still chuckling, he dropped forward, then started flipping his keys again, the metallic jangle breaking up the silence.

Lexi couldn't take talking about disappeared Jon anymore. "When does practice start anyway? Maybe I'll come watch, cheer you on."

"Not for months." Still holding the keys, Ash set his left hand on his right shoulder and swung his elbow up. "I didn't know you were interested in baseball."

Lexi straightened, arching her back. "It's the best sport to watch. A guy has to be really confident. It's not like football, where everyone's running around at the same time, hiding under those stupid helmets and pads while they smash into each other like idiots." She tilted her head, hoping to look casual as she tiptoed around, testing the waters. "Besides, I'm a member of the athletic boosters. We're all supportive of the players."

Ash frowned as he set the keys next to the milk carton.

"You know," she continued, artfully twisting a strand of hair around one pink acrylic nail, "we have that auction every fall. The one where you guys get to help us raise money for equipment by being someone's personal assistant for the day? Since you're the pitcher that kind of makes you the leader and —"

"Yeah, about that." The light went out of his eyes. "Being someone's personal ass is —" His cell's ringtone, an old song from The White Stripes, cut through his words. He checked the display. "Jon's mom. Again."

He slid Lexi an apologetic grin, answered with an adult-friendly 'hello', and immediately started reassuring Jon's mom that he hadn't heard anything from the guy. Not one word. Email. Or text.

She shifted away from Ash, taking in each carefully coordinated inch of the Carpenters' Home Channel kitchen. Yellow roses dotted the curtains and dishcloths, deep-green ivy crept up the walls. Tidy rows of white plates and matching mugs sat on the shelves. The desperately successful combination mocked her as minutes dragged by. Intentionally blocking out Ash's end of the conversation with Jon's mom, she stewed on the manageable part of her dilemma. The part that didn't threaten to tear her world apart. The way she saw it, there were two possibilities.

Get Ash on her list—significantly increase chances of replacing Taylor as the athletic boosters' president for next year.

Lose Ash to Monica—watch Monica accept the post. And the recognition and, more importantly, the instant respect that came with it.

The garage door opener clicked on, followed by the rattle of the door going up. Mrs. Carpenter. So much for using them being alone to her advantage. Despite what Ash said about his mom being understanding, Lexi knew having a mom around changed everything. Especially when it came to guys.

Lexi's cell vibrated. She checked the screen—her best friend, Jasmine Panjiwani, asking for a status update. She looked back at Ash, ready to offer him a flirty grin, but his gaze was focused on the other side of the kitchen where Mrs. Carpenter was coming in.

He covered the phone with his hand, speaking softly to his mom, "Jon's mom again." Glancing at Lexi, he frowned, adding, "Sorry, I guess this is gonna be a while. I'll get you tomorrow or something, okay?" He turned away, giving Jon's mom his full attention.

"Sure." This opportunity was over. She grabbed her bag then slid out of the chair, slowing only just enough to say hi to Mrs. Carpenter, but the woman cornered her.

"Isn't it awful?" she said, clutching a grocery bag. "Ashton and I, with his dad gone, I don't know what I'd do if he ran off like that. Left me all alone. Poor Mrs. Eagle." There was an awkward pause while Ash's mom stared off into space, thinking about God knows what. Then, just when Lexi thought she was going to get free, the woman leaned close enough to deliver a cloud of White Linen. "Are you and Ashton dating?"

Dating?

"Um, no." She glanced at Ash but he didn't seem to be paying attention to this super awkward moment. "We're just talking about school stuff."

"Oh. Well. That's nice." Mrs. Carpenter lowered the bag, took a relieved or disappointed—Lexi couldn't tell which—step back, and started unpacking the groceries. "You come over any time, dear."

Talk about weird.

Lexi called thanks over her shoulder as she rushed through the stiff, overdecorated living room.

Outside, she scurried to her embarrassing, beat-up blue Saturn parked by the curb. The car took two tries to get it started. Once the engine was rumbling, she switched the radio on, then pulled out onto Oak. Familiar houses blurred past and within ten minutes she was turning right, onto her street. The one street in picture-perfect Cherry Grove lined with shabby houses and punctuated by broken-down cars. Not even the charming fall trees made much difference. It was the section of town everyone else pretended didn't exist.

She parked on the side of the driveway closest to the neighbor's house, right next to their tattered basketball net. A cat screeched, the wiry hound dog across the street barked then howled. Some kids were shouting from a yard a couple houses down. It was the usual thing. Trying not to look at the drab ordinariness, she stomped through the crunchy leaves scattered across the walk and headed for her door.

No matter what it took—hiding secrets, avoiding reality, dealing with Monica—she'd get away from Cherry Grove. No way in hell was this place going to be her future.

Chapter Two

Another Day in Cherry Grove

Sunday night, Lexi sat cross-legged on the couch staring at the television, idly flipping through the lame basic cable channels. Weather, news, sports talk shows, reruns of stuff nobody really wanted to watch in the first place.

Her mom rattled around the kitchen, starting their usual late dinner. Probably Hamburger Helper or some other uninspired meal-in-a-box. "That surprise I told you about will take your mind off him—and those auction sign-ups."

Lexi never should have told her mom about waiting to hear from Ash, but she'd had to do something to distance her from talking about still-missing Jon. Just because her mom worked at the school superintendent's office, she thought she was part of everything. So she always wanted to talk about school, kids and the teachers.

"There's more to life than guys, honey," she said, ignoring Lexi's silence.

"Oh, really?" Lexi mumbled over the whine of the can opener.

She loved her mom, but the woman was a disaster when it came to men, relationships and understanding what mattered. And Lexi was past hoping things between her and her mom could be the way they had been before her father had died, or even right afterward, before Dale Welks had weaseled himself into the picture. Right after her dad had died, Lexi had felt important, needed. She'd helped her mom sort through his clothes and the other stuff he'd left behind. It had been sad, boxing things up and taking them to the Salvation Army donation place, but her mom had needed her then. During that time before Dale, the two of them had been close, spending weekend afternoons watching movies, baking or going to garage sales. It had been simple, ordinary stuff but it had been just the two of them.

Then along came Dale, filling her mom's head with a bunch of daydreams. Fantasies that he'd destroyed then rebuilt over and over for the past couple years. This time he'd been gone long enough that it seemed like he might actually be gone for good. Even though her mom couldn't see it, they were both better off without him. If he stayed gone long enough, maybe things could go back to the way they had been before.

Her mom gave the oven door a final push then joined Lexi in their small family room. "Could you put on the news for the weather?" she asked, dropping into her favorite, brown plaid chair. "Maybe you want to help with raking tomorrow after school? We could do it together when I get home. It might take your mind off—"

"I'll put the news on," Lexi sighed. "But I'll pass on raking leaves."

After stopping on channel seven, she tossed the remote onto the table and leaned forward to grab the notes for her US history quiz, but paused.

Familiar trees. And those benches.

Where?

Then she knew.

Morgan Park.

Speaking blandly, pointing over his shoulder, the newscaster continued with his update. "The body was spotted by a nearby resident who saw the man seated on the park bench around ten in the morning then again later when she went out to walk her dog. The woman approached the man, then called nine-one-one when he was not responsive."

The image of the reporter shifted to the side and a second reporter, back at the station, popped into view.

"The body has been identified as Mr. Filpot, Cherry Grove High's popular baseball coach."

Her mom gasped then mumbled something.

The reporter said more things that didn't register with Lexi, then concluded with, "I'm sure we'll be hearing more about this as additional information is released."

Coach Filpot dead?

As in, like, never coming back?

Lexi blinked. Her mom murmured something about the coach's poor family.

Dead was dead.

What'll happen to the player auction?

The stab of guilt that came on the heels of that thought made Lexi wince, but the question didn't go away.

Neither did the shivers that sent her heart skittering.

The next morning, outside science lab three, thick gray clouds smothered the sky, threatening to explode with plump pellets of rain. The oranges and yellows of the early-turning trees gleamed like liquid fire, and the branches swayed and spit leaves onto the ground. Inside the school, everyone hunched over their work, half awake, struggling along with the assignment. The whisper of conversation was light, even for first hour Monday morning. Thanks to Taylor's Twitter, Instagram and Facebook blitz, red and black 'school spirit' outfits acted as a constant reminder that Coach Filpot had died just the day before.

Lexi's sketchpad was covered with lousy attempts to recreate the microorganisms clinging to her microscope slide, and the drawings were getting worse by the minute. Each time she looked at the slide the stupid things blurred together, turning themselves into pinkish, shapeless blobs. How was she supposed to draw that? Somehow she had to get motivated. Every grade mattered and all those grades together were her ticket out.

Jasmine was perched on a tall stool across the lab table, her notes scattered over its enameled surface. She kept shuffling the papers around, putting them in order then rearranging them. She wasn't the only one showing signs of stress. All around the room people were halfheartedly flipping through textbooks, sitting with their chins low, and tapping their pencils against notebooks.

Jazz waved her hands. "This is ridiculous. Nobody's getting anything done. They should've canceled school," she whispered to Lexi.

Lexi twisted away from the microscope. Jazz's usually perfect ebony bob lay flat against her scalp, and the flawless makeup was missing from her thickly lashed, sable eyes. Not even her bright red, mini-cable cashmere twinset made her look decent.

"You guys still doing the auction?" she asked.

"Yeah," Lexi whispered back. "Taylor put up a post last night. It's still on. That's what Coach would've wanted."

"She's right." Jazz rolled her pencil across the black table, the tiny rattle loud in the hushed room. "At least they know what happened to Coach. He had a heart attack or something. But what about Jon? He could be hurt or—or—"

What could Lexi say that wouldn't freak Jazz out even more? Or, worse yet, reveal what she knew? "He hasn't really done anything since graduation. Maybe he just wanted some time to himself before he left for the navy. Isn't he supposed to leave around Thanksgiving?" Lexi offered, even knowing how lame she sounded.

"The cops are wrong, nobody knows anything. Alan and I talked to everyone on the team. Trust me, if there was someone who knew something we would have found it out." Jazz frowned and leaned forward. "It's not like him to go somewhere without telling anyone. And leave alone? No way."

Too true. Jon Eagle was the kind of guy who'd text his mom from a party to let her know when he'd be home. Not the kind to run off without telling anyone. But then again, how well can you ever really know someone?

"I called his house again this morning—still nothing. The cops aren't actually doing everything they can. They're just saying they are to shut people up." Jazz started pushing her papers around again. "We're going to add more stuff to the Facebook page we made, more pictures, and list the places where he hangs out."

Awesome.

A virtual milk carton.

Thinking of Jon's frantic mother, Lexi shoved her notebook across the table. "Good idea, maybe it'll help." She hopped down from the high stool in front of the microscope. "Go ahead and take your turn—everything I'm drawing sucks."

Jazz shrugged and changed seats. "Might as well try to get something done."

Lexi set her pathetic drawings aside, pulled out her chapter questions and flipped through the overloaded textbook. As the bright photographs and glossy diagrams flashed past, her attempts to concentrate were ruined by a pair of seniors speculating about Coach Filpot.

Dead Coach Filpot.

"It's wild, him dying like that. I could see him getting a heart attack running around, cussing out umpires, but not sitting on a park bench."

"What makes you so sure he had a heart attack? They didn't say how he died."

"What else could it be? He was sitting there, had a heart attack, and croaked."

One of them snickered. "Maybe that missing guy—Jon Eagle—killed him!"

"Yeah, Cherry Grove's own serial killer."

"Shut the hell up," a red-haired jock growled. "Not everyone around here is like morbid like you losers."

Other kids joined in and the room swelled with speculation. Some stupid, some grisly.

After a moment, a carefully pitched voice sliced through the chatter, worming its way straight into Lexi's ear. "Hi there. Aren't you the picture of the serious student?"

Her again. Dressed to get noticed in a snug black-and-red striped crewneck, skinny jeans and sweet ballet flats.

"Sorry. Don't have time to chat." Lexi scowled at Monica's peach-glossed smirk. "I'm busy getting a better grade than you. Again."

Monica leaned down and whispered in a candy-coated voice, "Well, I just wanted to let you know you can stop freaking out. I got a text from Jon."

Lexi dropped her pencil and looked up. But Monica wasn't looking at her. She was looking at the pair of guys behind them, glancing from one to the other. When she was finally done sucking up their admiration like she was Kim Kardashian or some other famous-for-being-famous wannabe, she looked back to Lexi, her expression saying *of course they love me*. It was the usual thing. Everyone loved perfect Monica Sanders.

Dr. Newberg, typical off-the-wall science teacher, drove that point home by smiling at Monica as he announced, "Time to pack up the equipment. Put your reports and slides on the front counter — be sure they're labeled with your name and lab number."

Once the scraping of stools against linoleum filled the room, Lexi grabbed Monica's arm. "Why aren't you telling anyone you talked to Jon?"

"I didn't talk to him. I got a text from him."

"Whatever. Why didn't you tell the cops?"

"He doesn't want me to," she replied, turning back to the guys who'd been staring at her, smiling at them with her glossy lips.

Relief battled with shock. Lexi stepped between Monica and the guys. "Why not?"

"How the hell should I know?" Monica raked her gaze across Lexi's face. "Stop looking like that—and don't you tell anyone either. Just be glad he's okay and keep your mouth shut. Worry about yourself. And your signatures."

Across the table, Jazz scowled at Monica's back as she finished packing up the microscope. After clicking the case shut, she hauled the clunky box off the table and headed to the storage closet, dodging the students already coming back then disappearing into a cluster by the closet door.

Jazz was an awesome friend, but every summer she went to Montreal to stay with her grandparents. If Jazz didn't go away every June, then Lexi never would've gotten mixed-up with Monica. But she had, so now she had to deal what she'd done with her. Ready to fight back, Lexi slipped on her own phony smile. "How're you doing with your signatures?"

"Better than you are, I'm sure," Monica replied, moving her phony expression back to her admirers, lowering her voice. "If you spend all your time trying to sign Ash I'll have the whole team on my list before he even considers texting you. Unless, of course," she looked up from under her mascara-coated lashes, "you finally decide to put out."

Lexi ignored the second dig as she studied Monica, committing the moment to memory so she could play it over and over in her mind, her very own YouTube clip. "Ash and I didn't waste time on texts, he just asked me over."

Monica scoffed. "So you aren't the school's biggest tease anymore? When did you find time to turn in your Lifetime Virgin membership card?" She laughed, throwing her head back dramatically as she strolled off, her suddenly sharp gaze a reminder to keep quiet.

At least keeping quiet was easier than being afraid.

"What's the big deal about the list anyway?" Jazz asked Lexi as they swerved through the hallway, dodging a group of students from AP Spanish selling raffle tickets for their annual trip to the Guatemalan rainforest. "You're already in the boosters. I get that you want another thing to put under extracurricular activities, but are you sure you want all that responsibility? I know if anyone can handle it you can, but still…"

"I'd be good at it," Lexi replied as they rounded the corner by the counseling offices and cut through the mob of anxious kids waiting to turn in their progress reports. They paused by one of the giant, rain-smeared windows to watch a series of lightning bolts slash across the sky, slicing through the autumn trees like bony fingers. Heavy thunder shook the building and churning gray clouds covered the sky.

"And that Monica," Jazz said, sliding a glance to Lexi after a particularly fierce flash of lightning. "What did she want? And why is she such an epic she-beast?"

Lexi avoided Jazz's gaze and lifted her finger to trace the lines of water streaming down the window. "Who knows what she wants? She's a freak."

"You got that right. No wonder she never has any friends." Jazz moved away from the window. "See ya at lunch."

Monica a she-beast? Jasmine didn't know the half of it. And she wasn't going to. And neither was anyone else.

Just as Lexi was about to turn the other way and head to history, she spotted the baseball team's freakiest but best-playing pair, second baseman Tony Jackson and shortstop Scott MacArthur.

She moved away from the wild storm outside as she smoothed her hair into place and, wearing her best you're-going-to-sign-for-me-now smile, called, "Hey, Shortie, hi, Spaz."

Spaz rolled up, tipping the brim of his oversize white Tigers cap so it covered one of his bright blue eyes. "Yo, Lexi, I done told you, it's S-Paz."

"I'm not calling you that. Not now. Not ever." Good God. But what else can you expect from a guy who put rims on a Jeep Wrangler?

"Why you hatin' on me like that?" He rolled his head one way then the other. "Why can't you show a brother some luv?"

Watching him run his fingers across the gleaming silver hat size sticker, she shook her head, held out her auction sheet and Bic. "Sign this."

"Due to the sad news on the streets, S-Paz and his boy aren't doin' buiznass today," Spaz said, reaching down to haul up his insanely huge jeans.

How could he not know that scene was so completely over? "Sign now and I won't remember that Pretty Ricky poster you had hanging in your locker all through middle school." Then, crossing her gaze to Shortie, she added, "I won't remember that dance when you and—"

"Gimme that." Shortie signed, then passed the sheet and made sure Spaz took care of business.

The whole incident was over in a matter of seconds.

"Thank you, boys," she called over the ringing bell, trotting down the almost empty hall.

Tiptoeing into history class, she scooted past the first two rows and tucked herself into her assigned seat.

Miss Crossman, perched on her desk in a horrible black and red polka-dot dress and looking as subdued as everyone else, leaned over to make eye contact. "Lexi?"

Lexi's heart thumped. She really did not need to get sent to the office. "Yeah?"

"The quiz has been postponed until tomorrow." She tapped the sheet of paper in her hands against her desk and added, "I was just telling everyone that Coach Filpot's funeral will be on Saturday." After saying some stuff about counseling available during lunch and after school, she started with where they'd left off the day before.

Lexi tried to get into whatever Miss C was saying about the oh-so-important Whiskey Rebellion, but the only thing rolling around her head was Jazz's question—what's the big deal about being president?

It'd be easy to convince her friend that she wanted the spot to make her look good. Everyone knew Lexi picked school activities based on how they'd look on college applications.

Everything she did—like adding to the ever-growing pile of college packets on her desk—she did to get closer to getting into the best school possible. Sure, having a degree would be great someday, but that stack on her desk represented something more important—her ticket out of Cherry Grove.

But the plain truth about the president's spot was that it'd give her instant respect. And it wasn't her future that fueled her desire for respect. It was her past. Back when she let losers—like Dale—take advantage of her and control her life.

A year ago, when she'd gotten her license, she'd figured out what a total manipulator her stepdad really was. It was obvious he hated losing control, because he'd taken every opportunity he could find to butt into her life. And ask questions.

Where was she going?

Who would be there?

Why did she want to hang out with them?

Each time he came up with another ridiculous concern, he'd share it with her mom. Eventually her mom had started thinking Dale knew what he was talking about. Why couldn't she see the only thing he cared about was wedging himself between them, keeping the two of them from being close the way they'd been before he'd shown up?

When he'd started taking those out-of-town jobs, Lexi had hoped things would get better between her and her mom, but they hadn't. Sure, they got to spend time together while he was away, doing mom and daughter stuff, but her mom constantly talked about him like he was still there, like he mattered. In a way he was there, because he always reappeared, claiming he had to sign in at the union local to see what companies were hiring welders. Every time he showed up, she welcomed him back as though his coming and going was normal, as though all husbands acted that way.

Lexi ran her finger down the edge of the desk, assuring herself for the thousandth time that she'd never let herself be treated like crap again. The first step to making that happen was getting named boosters' president. She'd start under Taylor during basketball season then take over completely in the spring. Next year things would be perfect. Her last year in Cherry Grove would be everything she wanted it to be. Why? The boosters' president was on top. Whatever she wanted—she got. Invitations, attention, best seats anywhere, rides to everywhere and most of all—no-questions-asked, just do-what-I-say—respect.

"What're you smiling about?"

The husky whisper came from the next row over. Outfielder Peter Archer—auction list prospect—had pulled his gaze away from the drizzle-spattered window.

Luck was on Lexi's side and this chance to sign up another player wasn't to be wasted. With practiced ease, she forced the raw emotions deep inside where they couldn't do damage, broadened her smile and angled over. "I'm thinking about you. And me."

Peter's grin was full of promise. "You think you can talk me into signing?" Heading into his third season, he knew the girls were in fierce competition to get the most signatures. He folded his arms across his faded Cherry Grove hoodie. "You won't get your chance till Friday night."

"We don't have school on Friday, so make it Thursday." Lexi gave him a slow once-over, admiring the way his long legs nearly hit the underside of the desk.

His smirk told her he noticed her looking and liked it. "Pick you up at eight?"

Lexi nodded, shifting her gaze back to Miss C and letting her smile drop. Progress, yes, but it wasn't him she was really after.

Chapter Three

Some Jokes Aren't Funny

Thursday night after dinner, shower steam swirled around Lexi like a protective cloud, pushing away the insecurities that threatened to cling every time she went out with a guy.

She'd gotten pretty good at keeping those annoying doubts at arm's length, but still, that look on a guy's face when he realized she really did mean no—sometimes it was hard to take. Not because she cared what they thought, but because it made them harder to handle.

At least with Peter they both knew she was after his signature. He'd see how much he could get. She'd give as little as possible.

Sure, the whole night might be a hassle, but in the end she'd get what she wanted.

Even after Lexi rinsed out her conditioner and shaved every possible place on her legs, she still had some extra time, so she covered her face with an orange facial mask then stretched across her bed, waiting for the mixture to do its thing.

"Lexi?" her mother called from behind the door. "Can I come in?"

Not the best time, but Lexi still couldn't completely give up on having a real relationship with her mom. Trying not to crack the mask, she replied through her teeth, "Sure."

Lexi lifted herself up as the door swung open.

Indescribably horrible pleated jeans and a garage sale sweatshirt. It was her mom's usual at-home uniform. Lexi could comment about the dreadful outfit, but why bother? Her mom would never change.

"Who're you going out with tonight?" she asked, sliding the stack of college information packets aside and propping herself against the white wicker desk. Photographs of booster girls were scattered across the glass top behind her.

"Peter Archer. He plays baseball."

Lexi added that second piece of information not because it mattered, but because for some inane reason her mom loved it when she went out with the jocks. Maybe she thought they came from good homes.

Better families.

Translation — richer families.

"You'll bring him in so I can meet him?" she asked, a hopeful light in her hazel eyes.

Lexi lifted herself onto her elbows and took in her mom's second-hand clothing disaster. The pants were the second reason the answer to that would be no.

The first?

The last time she'd brought a guy in for her mom to meet, she'd fussed over him like he was some actor in a lame TV show and she was one of those ladies who served lemonade and homemade cookies. Her mom always acted the same way with Dale, hanging around him like he needed constant special attention. Maybe she thought treating guys that way made her attractive, but it really just made her look ridiculous and, even worse, easier to step on.

But Lexi couldn't say all that. "If we have time, I'll bring him in."

"That'll be fine," she said, nodding vaguely as she gazed around the room. Eventually she came back around to look at Lexi. "How's everyone at school feeling about Coach Filpot?"

"Bummed." Thinking about the guys in science earlier that week, she added, "Some are saying stupid stuff but most everyone still feels bad, especially because it was so sudden."

Her mom nodded again. "That staff are shaken up too. I've been trying to call Mrs. Filpot all week, but she isn't answering the phone. I left some voicemails, but well…" Her mom picked up one of the group photos. "Can't say that I blame her, you know, for not wanting to talk to anyone. I remember when after…"

Lexi wanted to encourage her mom to talk about those times but after the week she'd had, didn't have the strength. Dealing with Monica, worrying about getting the signatures, and the thing with Jon had her stretched so tight even the smallest emotion might make her lose it. She pushed herself all the way up. "Have to rinse."

"I won't keep you." Her mom tipped her head, that hopeful light starting to shine in her eyes. "I'm sure you want to look good for your guy."

Your guy.

Oh please.

Her mom put the picture down, straightened it so it was perfectly in line with the others, then stood, looking over suddenly, the pain of thinking about losing her first husband gone. "Don't forget about the surprise I promised."

The real smile that spread across Lexi's face felt strange but good. "Oh, right, I haven't."

"Great."

Then the moment was gone.

After her mom started down the stairs, Lexi headed for the bathroom to rinse off the mask and dig her scented moisturizer from the linen closet. Glancing at her too-short legs and flat butt, she knew she didn't have a perfect figure, but compared to the other girls at school she looked as good.

Except Monica.

Monica stood about three inches taller. With perfect, eye-catching C boobs that most girls had to pay for with their graduation money.

Everything about Monica looked perfect.

Witness the partial list — National Honor Society, student government treasurer, regular office volunteer, consistent doer of all things right. All the teachers liked her. Why wouldn't they? She did everything they told her to and managed to do — or look like she was doing — the right thing even when they didn't.

Family-wise, she also looked perfect. Both her parents were accountants and they all lived together in an awesome brick Georgian in the Briarwood subdivision, right across the street from Zoë Weinberg, whose mom was the real estate queen who owned practically half of Cherry Grove.

Lexi had the grades — better than Monica's, in fact — but not that complete perfection. Perfection so plastic it would snap if tested. But Lexi wasn't about to do anything to test it, because the nasty secrets hiding inside Monica's life were so foul they could ruin them both. And that instant respect Lexi craved? Not a chance. And losing that would be just the start.

Thank God Jon was okay.

After tossing the lotion back into the closet, Lexi sprayed herself with the matching body spray, promised herself she'd stop obsessing over Monica — at least for the night — then marched back to her room. While she was pushing in silver hoop earrings, the bass of Ke$ha blaring out of Peter's mounted speakers nearly shook the framed photos off her desk. Then the street fell silent, followed by the thud of a car door.

No way was she going to put Peter through the Ridiculous Pampering Experience. She tied her shrunken pink hoodie around her waist as she tiptoed down the steps. The corny sound of laugh track TV floated in from the other room as Lexi crept out of the door and hurried to the curb.

Peter had climbed out of his black H2 and stood on a corner of the leaf-covered grass with his hands shoved into his tattered Red Monkey jeans, tugging them even lower on his narrow hips. He grinned. Or was it a leer? "I don't think I've ever picked up a girl who was actually ready when I got there."

"No big deal," she replied, jogging toward him. "I put on some clean clothes" — she flipped her hands back, inviting his appraisal — "and here I am."

With the band of his black Hanes cutting a path across his tight stomach, and his sun-bleached curls covering one eye, he looked damn good. But then his personality ruined the moment because instead of saying something decent, he stared at her boobs then checked out her crotch.

Lexi liked knowing she could get a guy's attention, but those looks bugged her. Sure, it was normal to look at people but a guy didn't have to be gross about it. Like each guy had his own pair of invisible X-ray goggles, and he spent his whole day looking for some girl to test them out on.

What could she do with that constant annoyance that made her want to tell the guy to F off?

Ignore it.

Because she refused to let Peter, or anyone else, know she was anything but cool with the attention. How weak would that be?

Finally done staring, Peter fell back, climbed up into the seat, slid behind the steering wheel and kicked over the engine. He tapped his phone and Taylor Swift burst from the speakers. He grinned over at her through the open passenger window.

Good God, how predictable.

Lexi climbed in anyway.

The heat of summer had come back and hot moist air rushed in as he swung out away from the curb. Within a minute they were turning off her rundown street, moving away from the battered houses of her neighbors. As the corner house grew smaller in the side mirror, recklessness flooded Lexi's veins.

That feeling was nothing new. Neither was the thought that came right after it—one day she'd leave and never come back.

At the E-Wood Multiplex lot, Peter wedged his H2 between a green Impala and some decades-old, wood-trimmed minivan, slid out and waited with his hands shoved in his back pockets as Lexi climbed down.

Behind him, the giant white brick theater stretched out for a whole block. Families, couples, clusters of friends milled about, pouring in and out of the glass doors. Above the rows of doors, blue and purple neon lights circled the movie listings.

The glittering night was just right. Except that Peter was an ass. Which was too bad, because standing there with the sun falling behind him, his face all shadowed and angular, he looked hot. Like an Abercrombie boy toy.

But he was an ass, so once she was out he looped around behind her, bent down and flattened his palms on her butt, squeezing her butt cheek as he shoved her toward the entrance.

Forcing a laugh, she scooted away. "What do you want to see?"

"You plan to watch the movie?" he asked, grabbing at her again and laughing at his own stupidity.

The usual Peter moves.

They picked the show with the shortest line, some futuristic army thing, then found seats in the back. Lexi tossed her sweater onto the armrest and Peter stretched his arm behind her, resting his hand on her shoulder. It was cozy but not too much, so she settled back.

Actual emotions flickered in his eyes for a second, and he asked, "Heard anything new about Jon?"

Monica's face flashed in Lexi's mind. "No."

"What?" He tapped her shoulder. "What were you going to say?"

"Nothing." Lexi rubbed her nose, hiding the twitchy feeling taking over her face. "Why would I know anything?"

"I don't know." Peter shrugged, his mouth tight. "Well, it's weird. He's been gone over a week."

Like she hadn't been counting the days.

He slouched. "You met the new kid?"

Thinking about the person just added to her homeroom, Lexi asked, "The girl with the mini-fro?"

"No." He leaned closer and started picking at the seams of Lexi's tee. "Some new kid Ash is hyped about. He says the guy played in the Little League World Series, so he's really, really good. He's going to catch for us."

She shook her head. "Nope, I was over at Ash's the other night, he didn't say anything about him."

"He's got some weird name. Zen? Teke?"

A memory flickered in Lexi's mind but fizzled out. "You sure he started school already?"

Peter's hand stopped moving. "Why, you going to corner him with your list?"

Lexi pulled her arms across herself. "A name's a name."

"You girls. But as long as you're willing to put out, I don't have a problem with it."

Lexi rolled her eyes.

Peter leaned still closer and whispered, "I'll make sure you like it."

"I'm not doing that," she whispered back.

He grabbed her shoulder. "Don't worry, I know what you want."

Was he playing around? Or serious?

The turn-off-your-cell cartoon started, and Lexi relaxed into the soapy-smelling cloud swirling around Peter. Even if it was Axe, it smelled pretty good. At least as long as the movie was going he couldn't say any more annoying stuff. The previews dragged on, but once the movie started, she got into it. About forty-five minutes in, her cell started vibrating. She ignored it, but it kept going on and off, practically shaking itself out of her pocket.

Five texts. Boyfriend drama. Jazz freaking out about Alan. Lexi leaned over to Peter, whispered, "Be right back." She scooted down between the seats. Once she was in the aisle, she pulled her cell out and hit 'Call'.

"Hi." Jazz came on before the first ring finished. "Um, yeah. So. How's it going with Peter?"

"Fine. Okay." It was nice of her to ask, of course, but they both knew that wasn't why she'd called. "What's going on with Alan?"

"Are you in the theater?"

"No. Well, I was, but I came out in the hall to answer."

There was a beat of nothing, then, "He's acting really weird about Jon, and I—"

A crowd of people started pouring out of the theater across from the one she'd just come out of, so Lexi moved to the end of the hall and stood by a plate-glass window looking out at the side of the parking lot. "Jazz? What?" Lexi watched some minivans roll through the rows. "Are you okay?"

"Yeah." Jazz sniffed a couple times. "I don't want to go into it now, while you're supposed to be hanging out with Peter." She laughed a bit, then, sounding more like herself, added, "I know you have the list to deal with. Can you just call me when you're done?"

"Sure." Thinking about Peter's attitude, she added, "He's either going to sign or he's not, so it won't take long."

Jazz started to say something but stopped and fell silent again. A group vaguely familiar guys from school passed by on the other side of the window. They were pushing and shoving one another and doing some kind of silly karate chops, but laughing so hard they could barely lift their legs. They looked so ridiculous, Lexi almost laughed herself.

Finally, after Jazz sniffed again, she said, "Thanks. But don't hurry for me. Really, I'm okay."

The kicking guys were out of view now, and the lot was empty of people close enough to watch. "You wouldn't have called if it didn't matter," she said. "Right?"

"I know. Thanks. Bye." And she was gone.

Lexi spun around, took a step forward and stopped. Monica. Always in the wrong place at the right time.

"Hi, Lexi," she said, sticking her hip out as she leaned her shoulder against the wall. Some of her curls swung forward, some settled prettily behind her back. "Having fun?" she asked, smirking in her usual arrogant way.

Lexi resisted the urge to look her over and check out each tiny detail of her perfect outfit. Monica would not miss the once-over. She never missed anything. So Lexi kept her eyes steady, focused on Monica's as she casually slid her phone into her back pocket then stuffed her hands into her front pockets. "Whatever."

"Not a very nice attitude," Monica said, so softly it was almost a caress.

Lexi took a step back. "Maybe I'm not a very nice person."

Monica rolled back against the wall, shoving her breasts out as she lifted her eyebrows. "That's not the way I remember it."

"Like I said" — Lexi pulled her hands from her pockets and flipped them, emphasizing her pretend lack of concern — "whatever."

Monica made a point of looking down at Lexi, her natural few inches of additional height made even more thanks to her heeled boots. "You here alone?" she asked.

Lexi hated herself for not simply walking away. She'd didn't owe Monica anything. She didn't have to stand there and put up with Monica's smug attitude. But the truth was, Monica had some *thing*, a pull Lexi just couldn't back away from. "No." She tipped her shoulder slowly, mimicking a cute move she'd stolen from Monica herself. "I'm here with a guy."

Monica laughed, the noise sudden and aggressive. "I know." She nodded toward the theater Lexi had come out of. "I saw you come in with Peter. How's that going? He sign yet?" She laughed more, the delicate features of her face distorting into an expression Lexi was pretty sure nobody but her ever saw. "Did anyone sign for you yet?"

It was Lexi's turn to lift her eyebrows. She wasn't about to let Monica know she was the least bit shaken up. No way would she mention the second-string players — or even Spaz and Shortie — that she'd already signed. Better to keep the other girl wondering. Off balance. Better yet, away from her.

"Nothing to say?" Monica shook her head, her glossed lips all twisted, her breasts pressed against the typically tight sweater. "Didn't think so."

Lexi's patience snapped. "I'm not a whore like—"

"Yes?" Monica stood up, came forward and looked down Lexi's shirt. "You aren't a whore like me? You sure about that? You never used somebody to get what you wanted?"

Lexi brushed past the other girl and stalked back to the theater. As soon as the door swung shut, she stopped walking to stand just inside the dark room. After a few seconds her breathing started to slow and the tingle of anger and fear faded enough that she'd be able to pretend she was fine. The last thing she needed was Peter asking her a bunch of questions.

Ready to face him, she moved into the theater. Everyone was laughing when she came in, their heads bobbing all over the place. One guy in her row was even kicking. His foot connected solidly with her shin and he mumbled sorry. Lexi mumbled no problem and rushed to her seat, a sweet 'sorry I took so long' for Peter forming in her mouth.

But she didn't get a chance to use it because he was gone. Her sweater was right where she'd left it, but his seat was empty.

Some girl yelled, "Get out of the way, people are trying to watch a movie," so Lexi dropped into her seat and looked around to see if Peter had moved. She didn't spot him, so she slumped down.

Maybe he'd gone to the bathroom.

Or went looking for her?

She twisted, looking around as best she could. Was he in a different seat? Moved to play a joke on her? Went out and came back in and got lost?

A while later, she was still in the same position. Her heart was hammering and stomach was starting to churn.

He wasn't coming back.

What kind of loser ditched someone at the movies?

Lexi pulled out her phone and stared at the screen. Jazz was a mess. She didn't want to add to her stress by asking her to come get her. Lexi sent a 'can you come get me' text to her mom. After she hit 'Send', she looked around again, trying to see if Peter was staring at her, laughing.

He wasn't. She was sure he'd left.

She could send him a message and tell him what an asshole he was, but why give him the satisfaction of knowing he'd gotten to her? Whatever his agenda was, she wanted no part of it.

Lexi slipped on her sweater, got up, wove back to the aisle and headed for the door. Once in the hall, she checked her phone. Nothing from her mom. She tried calling, listening to all five rings before the voicemail went on. She clicked off without leaving a message.

Even though she knew it was pointless, Lexi went to the concession area and made a circle. Kids carrying popcorn, couples holding hands, groups of girls walking together with their faces tipped down to the phones in their hands.

No Peter.

She tried her mom again. No answer.

With no other choice, she called Jasmine, who answered right away.

"Peter ditched me. Can you come get me at the E-Wood?"

There was a pause, then, "He what?"

"He left while I was out in the hall. I know it sounds ridiculous but it's true. He left me here. By myself."

"Are you sure he left?" she asked, her voice rising. "Maybe he went to the bathroom."

Lexi grumbled then replied, "It's been, like, twenty-five minutes."

"That doesn't make any sense at all. Did you guys have an argument or something?"

"I know it doesn't make sense and no we didn't have an argument. We were watching the movie." *Until you called*. She didn't add that. No point making Jazz feel like crap for some stupid thing Peter did.

Always the reasonable one, Jazz kept her cool, stayed silent for a few more seconds before asking, "Maybe he got sick or something. Did you go look for his car?"

"No." Lexi ducked through the concession stand crowd and started walking toward the exit. "I feel so stupid, I should've thought of that."

"You were probably too busy being pissed."

Lexi hopped off the sidewalk, took four strides into the lot and saw a mud-spattered blue Jetta instead of Peter's H2. Her blood pressure skyrocketed.

"Yeah. It's gone."

"All right. What a total ass. I'll be there as fast as I can, but it'll take a few because I have to sneak out the back — don't ask, I'll explain when I get there. Wait by the side near the road, I'll pull up there."

"Thanks, Jazz." Lexi clicked off, took one last pointless look around the parking lot, then headed back to the side of the theater. As she turned the corner, she caught a glimpse of someone rounding the corner at the other end. Curly dark hair, long legs made even longer by high-heeled boots, and that unmistakable stiff, quick walk.

Monica.

What the hell was she up to?

But with that girl there was no telling. Follow her? She wanted to but the risk of being spotted wasn't worth it. Better to get the hell out of there as quickly as possible. Lexi dropped to the ground and leaned against the white brick, waiting for Jazz, telling herself again that all this effort would be worth it. Once she was named boosters' president, she'd get Monica out of her face, never have to put up with being ditched again, and be at the top of everything in Cherry Grove that mattered.

Chapter Four

There's No Place Like Home, Thank God

About twenty minutes later, Jazz pulled up. Lexi scanned the area to make sure Monica wasn't still around, spying on her or who knows what else, then climbed into Jazz's car.

"Hey," she said, then slammed the door. "Thanks for rescuing me."

"Of course. Thanks to you for listening to me about Alan." Jazz pulled away from the curb and headed toward the less hectic back section of the theater parking lot. "After I thought about it, I realized Peter left you there because you stepped out to talk to me."

Lexi shrugged and said, "Guys are jerks." She picked through the jumble of pens and lip glosses in the bottom of her bag until she found her house keys. "You going to be able to sneak back in?"

"Yeah." Jazz hit the gas and zoomed out into traffic. "I just have to remember to get up early to put the ladder away."

"Sorry about that. I don't want you getting in trouble because of me." Lexi ran her finger along the car door handle then looked out to the road in front of them. "I tried my mom first but she didn't answer."

"You called her?"

"Yeah." She squeezed the keys in her fist. "And texted."

Jazz frowned. "Maybe she's asleep."

"It's not even eleven yet." Lexi could hear the hurt in her own voice.

Jazz turned right, taking them closer to Lexi's section of town. "No big deal about the ladder. It's not like I haven't snuck out every other night this week." She tucked her hair behind her ears. "I think part of what's bugging Alan is that my dad is being all crazy about Jon disappearing, like it means there's some serial killer on the loose. Like every guy from school is a potential madman, including Alan, who my dad has known for like forever."

"It is weird, Jon being gone and staying gone," Lexi said, meaning every word.

Jazz pulled up in front of Lexi's house and put the car in park. "Everyone's saying that."

Lexi scanned the street. Porch lights cast an uneven yellow light across the hedges and piles of leaves. She looked at her front door, wondering again why her mom hadn't even responded. Too bad there wasn't sort of parent halfway between hers and Jazz's. Some kind of normal person who trusted their kid but looked out for them at the same time.

"Hey," Jazz said, snapping Lexi out of her thoughts. "What time is Filpot's funeral?"

Another difficult subject. There were just too many lately. "Three o'clock. I'll drive if you want. Pick you up at two?"

Jazz nodded, the side of her face flashing bright as a pickup truck rambled by.

Lexi shoved open the car door, waved at Jazz and went up the walk, kicking through the latest layer of leaves. Jazz backed out, the lights of her VW cutting across the doorway as Lexi went inside. The still house swallowed her as she padded through the dark living room. A familiar scent drifted under her nose, but the irritation that lingered from dealing with crazy, annoying Monica and Peter ditching her scattered her attempts to figure out what it was.

What a complete waste of a night. Next time she'd get the guy to sign first.

She stepped softly up the stairs, pausing at the top landing to look at her mom's closed door. There had been a time when her mom actually listened, made her feel better when bad stuff happened.

But those times were over.

Her gaze shifted to the doorway of her own room where her bed, visible beneath the window, waited. The rumpled pink chenille cover had been smoothed, her matching throw pillows carefully arranged. The usual trail of clothes from her closet to dresser — gone. A basket of folded laundry stood in its place.

Why her mom had suddenly turned into Martha Stewart, Lexi had no idea. But if she was in one of her everything-is-perfect moods, talking about anything real was definitely out of the question. Once inside her room, Lexi silently pressed her door shut, tossed her bag into her chair, then threw herself across her bed and stared at the shadowed ceiling.

Peter, ditching her.

Monica, always in her face. Reminding her of all the stupid stuff they'd done over the summer.

Jon, running off and making them keep his secret. Yes, she could tell what she knew. But one secret would lead to another. And another. And another, until the sickening truth came out. And Lexi couldn't let that happen.

What the hell? How much could one person take? Crying might make her feel better, less out of touch, less clueless, but she'd had so much practice holding back her feelings tears wouldn't come.

Why hadn't her mom answered her calls?

A genuine tear slid down Lexi's cheek, rolled past the corner of her lips. Another followed. She sat up, pulled in a deep breath and told herself to stop, but the tears kept coming.

Crying didn't make her feel better, it made her pathetic. Really, it wasn't that big a deal having some idiot you don't really like walk out on you. And Jon? Whatever stupid game he was playing didn't have anything to do with her. He was okay, that was all that mattered. She swiped away the tears and dropped back onto her lace pillows.

On the other side of the door, the creak of hallway floorboards was followed by a soft knock.

"Hi, honey." Her mom inched the door open, peering in, a vague smile on her mouth.

The sound of her mom's voice chased away some of the anger and embarrassment, and for a second Lexi let go of her indispensable self-control.

She sat up, reached for her mom, ready to tell her everything, but stiffened when she saw the other face in the doorway. The scent of burnt solder downstairs.

Her straightened room. Floorboards that only creaked under his weight.

She should've already known he was there.

Back, ready to worm his way into every hole of their lives.

"Remember, I told you I had a surprise," her mom said, typically oblivious to what was actually going on.

Lexi's tears turned into anger and through the haze of her mind she heard her stepfather's low husky whisper, her mom's light giggle. The sounds crawled deep inside her, tearing at her heart.

No more.

Desperate, she scooted into the corner, bracing herself by pulling the throw pillows to her sides.

Don't look at them.

Pretend they aren't there.

Together. Acting like everything is okay.

But the overhead light blinked on, exposing her so she couldn't deny their existence.

"Honey? Aren't you happy to see Dale?" She stepped into the room, the scent of her vanilla-and-pear lotion filling the air. "What's wrong? Didn't you have a nice time?"

Hollow laughter struggled up Lexi's throat. "That jerk ditched me, and you didn't answer my text or calls."

Silence swelled in the room, filling every nook. The quiet was so thick Lexi could have sworn she could hear her own heart beating.

"Honey?" her mom said after a minute, tugging at the flannel bathrobe she'd been wearing since before Lexi's dad died. "What do you mean he ditched you?"

"Left, Mom. Like, got in his car and drove away without me."

"I thought you were with Peter?" she said, backing away from Lexi as though she didn't understand, as though it was Lexi who'd done something wrong.

"Peter? Peter who?" Dale asked.

Lexi squeezed her eyes shut, wishing them both away, but of course they were still there, bathed in bright light, when she lifted her lids.

Her mom was leaning into the doorjamb but Dale was inching forward, the ashy scent that followed him everywhere getting stronger.

Hoping it would hold him back, she offered, "Peter, a guy on the baseball team."

"Peter Archer?" Dale said.

Of course he remembered the players.

Dale crept closer, pushing his dull brown hair off his forehead. "You need to tell us exactly what happened."

Lexi tipped sideways, pleading silently to her mom, but she was staring fretfully at Dale's gray terry cloth-covered back, letting him take control—as always. Even after being gone all that time.

To keep herself from having a complete internal meltdown, Lexi explained everything that had happened as quickly as possible. Once she'd finished, Dale said nothing to her, turning instead to her mom. "It's a good thing I came back when I did."

"Honey, I-I'm so sorry I— We didn't hear the phone. We were—" Her mom's face crumpled, her gaze shifting to Dale, who turned back to Lexi.

"You look all right now," he said.

"But it must've been terrible. Are you sure you're okay?" Her mom shuffled in but stayed behind her beloved Dale as she clutched the collar of her robe. "You want some cocoa? Want to talk some more?"

And endure more of Dale the pompous loser?

Not in a million years.

"I'm fine," Lexi said, ignoring all of her mom's questions. "I just want to go to sleep."

Her mom whispered to Dale, the light vanished, the door closed.

Lexi crawled under the covers with her clothes still on, until, eventually, sweet sleep swept her away.

Outside her door, the floorboards creaked under heavy footsteps.

Chapter Five

Can You Keep a Secret?

Friday afternoon, after two mind-burning hours in one of the beige-walled Cherry Grove Library study carrels, Lexi steered along the careful curves of the Fairview Ridge subdivision south of town. The dusty scent of fall leaves and freshly cut grass came in through her open windows, floating in with high-pitched kid laughter and the thump of a basketball hitting the driveway. Yeah, it was the same stuff as in her neighborhood, but out here, away from beat-down buildings and small, old houses, it was better. Much better.

Lexi pulled up in front of Taylor's bragalicious McMansion, tumbled out and leaped over the piles of leaves along the curb. People in Fairview didn't do ordinary things like bag leaves. They heaped them into the street and waited for the service trucks to come by and suck them up with a giant vacuum. Very tidy.

Lexi would rather have stayed at the library than come to this boosters' meeting, but her future depended on attending. So there she was, standing on Taylor's porch wearing her extra long, burgundy campus sweater, matching headband and All Stars, and pretending not to be the girl who'd been ditched in the middle of a movie.

Mr. Lawton swung open the ultra-fancy wooden front door before she rang the bell. Compared to other dads around Cherry Grove, he was all right. Friendly enough to not be awkward but didn't ask a bunch of tedious questions or pretend to be cool by talking about music. "Go on upstairs, Lexi," he said, waving his steaming U MICH mug toward the dark steps at the back of the house. "I think the girls are just getting started."

It was an expected Cherry Grove place, matched seating arrangements and color-coordinated knickknacks picked out by decorators. Huge windows that showed off the landscaped yard. Nothing personal or homey about it. Except the family photos in gleaming silver frames covering the piano. Those offered up a couple decades of winning at everything and always being the best.

Lush oriental rugs silenced Lexi's steps, even the stairs were quiet. It was like she wasn't even there. But she was—and so was Andrea MacNeil, because her voice was coming from Taylor's room.

"I can't believe he died sitting right there in the park."

Lexi paused outside the door. Sweet-faced Betty Ann Thompson, the only other freshmen in the boosters, added, "Well, geez. He was eighty or something. He was bound to die sometime."

"Peter Archer's mom and my mom have been helping Mrs. Filpot," Andrea said. "That lady is out of her mind. So they've pretty much been planning everything. Coach's wife probably just wants to cry her eyes out."

A pang of resentment hummed through Lexi. Her mom had reached out to Mrs. Filpot right away, before any of the other moms in Cherry Grove, and been rejected every time. Apparently the coach's wife had been waiting to be helped by the right people, like Mrs. MacNeil and Betty Ann's mom.

"Anyway," Andrea kept right on going, even though nobody was responding to her, "Do we really have to wear black? You guys are all going, right? Are we going to sit together?"

"I read some new stuff on Jon's Facebook page," somebody else said, ignoring Andrea's questions. "There's a list of places he likes to go, you know, to eat and stuff."

Murmurs followed. Debate about whether or not they had to wear black was cut into by more speculation about Jon and gossip about Mrs. Filpot losing it.

Lexi couldn't make out all the words, but she didn't need to. They all wanted details.

Information.

Monica's voice sliced through the chatter. "Yes, we have to wear black. Of course Mrs. Filpot is upset. Her husband died. Yes, we are sitting together. For unity and support. And the only thing we can do about Jon is be supportive of his family, stop spreading rumors, and let the cops know if we see him."

It was Monica's last comment that made the pang of resentment turn hard and settle deep inside Lexi.

The only thing.

Aside from telling the truth, yeah, keeping your mouth shut is the option.

Next came Zoë Weinberg's faint voice, so light and airy she practically sounded like some phone sex girl. "Monica's right, and going on about everything will only make us all feel worse. And nobody wants that. Right?"

If Lexi didn't quit stalling, Monica was going to totally take over. Lexi shook off the resentment, slid in, said hi with a bright face—not the expression of a girl who came from the wrong side of town and had too many things to hide—and took a spot on the bed, curling up against Taylor's lemon-yellow headboard. She set down her bag, fluffed out her hair, and did her best to look natural and carefree like everyone else.

Taylor, wearing a lagoon blue Speedo tracksuit, sat on the way-too-flowery cushion inside her huge window seat. She swept back her uncurled red hair and looked around the room to make sure everyone was focused on her. Once she was sure she had everyone's complete attention, she set her hands on her legs and leaned forward. "Okay, let's get started."

The meeting began with roll call and a list of what they'd talked about at the last meeting. Lexi needed to listen to Taylor, but all she could hear was the ugly rattle of her stepfather's voice. And the thick sound of her mother's weak silence.

Sad but true fact for the day—not even Peter's stupidity or worry about Jon or grief for Mrs. Filpot could keep her mind from circling back to Dale Welks.

Back, when he should have stayed gone.

How could her mom stay with a man who abandoned her, then wandered back like a stray dog? That crap he handed out about having to take work out of town, it couldn't be true. There had to be jobs around Cherry Grove. It was a big place, after all. And there were nearby cities that had to have work too.

The boosters meeting went on. Lexi sat silent, reminding herself that she needed to stay involved, yet unable to do more than keep that ready-willing-and-able smile firmly in place.

She managed a purposeful nod a couple times and even laughed when one of the girls made a joke. All the while, bits of discussion drifted around, Lexi half-listening.

"The coach would want this…"

"…the team…"

"Next year…"

A ring of laughter here, a choked giggle there, then one by one girls started checking their phones and talking about Peter. The noise kept rising, getting higher in pitch as panic increased and guesses got wilder. Thank God none of the ideas included her or the theater.

"Okay, exactly how many people got a text asking about Peter?" Zoë asked, waving her glam pink-covered phone.

Andrea, Betty Ann and other girls raised their hands.

"Me too," Zoë said, still holding up her cell. "He's supposed to be helping his mom set things up, and she's pissed because he's blowing it off."

"I bet he's getting drunk with Troy."

"Those two are idiots."

"What about you, Lexi?" Monica asked. "Did you get a text about Peter?"

Monica's dark eyes gleamed, her glossy lips pulling into that smile that sent chills down Lexi's spine. This time the chills were accompanied by a wave of anger because obviously she knew about Peter leaving her at the theater. Considering Monica and what she'd do for guys, she'd probably set the whole thing up. Told him if he ditched Lexi, she'd give him what he wanted for the signature.

No way was she going to give the other girl any satisfaction. Flashing a smile so sweet she could be on the cover of an ACT prep book, Lexi turned to Monica with a soft voice everyone would hear, but a nasty stare only Monica would see. "Nope. No texts. And last time I saw him, he was fine. Just fine. And smiling."

Monica turned away, acting as though Lexi hadn't said a thing. Taylor cut through the chatter with a reminder that they had stuff to get done. Phones dropped lower, but the damage was done — none of the girls focused on the agenda and each kept glancing down for more information. For Lexi, the rest of the meeting blurred by in a slow haze. Most of her effort was spent on not looking at Monica. In the end, there was a vote. They agreed to sit together at Coach's funeral and the auction date stayed the same.

Once Taylor called the meeting officially over, all the phones came up at once and everyone started talking about Peter. There was no new information, just all the girls trying to piece together what they knew. Oddly, nobody mentioned him going to the movies. Had he kept that a secret? Why?

From the corner of her eyes, Lexi watched Monica. She was cozying up to Taylor, speaking so softly Lexi couldn't hear what the two of them were discussing. Knowing Taylor, it was anything but gossip. Which meant Monica was doing what Lexi should be doing, getting more involved in the work and doing whatever she could to help organize the auction.

Planning to text Taylor later to ask what she could do, Lexi offered everyone a wave, said bye, and slipped back down the silent steps.

Twenty minutes later, as Lexi was turning into her driveway, her phone chirped. Her stir-crazy stress completely evaporated when she checked the display.

"Hi, Ash." She pictured his cute dimple and intense eyes.

"Hey there," he said, his yummy voice husky.

She climbed out and headed up the walk, which, thanks to her mom and not ever-lazy Dale, was no longer covered with leaves.

"You doin' anything tonight?"

Lexi smiled, leaned onto the front door and pushed it open. But what she found on the other side made the grin vanish. Dale, stretched across the couch, flipping through a stack of papers clutched in his soot-stained hands. His dirty boots were kicked off on the floor and his feet, covered in grubby white socks, rested on the arm of the couch. Clods of dirt dotted the rug. And that smell, the sooty, ashy scent that followed him everywhere, floated around the room.

Swallowing hard, carefully disregarding him as she strolled past, she replied softly to Ash, "Just hangin' out."

But Dale wasn't about to return the favor by ignoring her too. From the corner of her eye, she saw him sweep the papers aside, set his feet on the floor and lean forward.

"Lexi," he said, putting a threat in his tone, trying to stop her from going up the stairs.

She cringed, struggling to keep the ugly tension out of her voice when she whispered into the phone, "Hey, can I call you back in a minute?"

"You okay?" After a second of silence, Ash came back, "I'm coming over to get you in a half hour. Okay?"

Lexi sensed Dale closing in behind her, felt a fog of tension settle across her shoulders then drift down her spine. *Not now!*

She opened her mouth to say '*sure, of course*' to Ash, but he'd clicked off. Lexi tucked her phone into her palm, praying he wouldn't try to snatch it away from her.

"Who was that?"

Lexi pretended to be relaxed and casual as she brushed off Dale's question. "Is my mom around?"

"Who was that on the phone?" he asked, angling back and folding his bony arms across his chest.

Answering might be the only way to shut him up. "Ash Carpenter."

Moving forward, he forced her to smell that scent again as he asked yet another annoying question. "Why was he calling you?"

"Because he's my friend." Lexi dropped her phone into her bag, took a step up, feeling some of the tension fade as she got father away from him and found her nerve. "What's it to you?"

Dale set his hand on the banister, searching her face. "The school's athletic director asked me to step in for Coach Filpot. For this season, maybe next too, if things work out."

Why did he think she cared? "Whatever."

"Ash's a good player. Solid. Dedicated. Not all kids are like that, you know?"

She took another step back, and because it made her feel stronger, she let the irritation snap in her eyes and voice. "Do you want something?"

"I've talked to your mother about that deal the two of you made." Amazingly, his thin lips curved down even farther. "The curfew?"

She forced herself to breath naturally. "What about it?"

"With Jon still missing and everything that's going on with you, I think she's starting to see what I've been telling her. Good grades or not, you need a curfew. It's what's right."

Like you'd know what's right.

Lexi turned away, replying over her shoulder as she marched up the stairs, "My curfew is none of your business."

"I'm making it my business," he called back. "You don't seem to understand that—"

Lexi rushed to her room, cutting off his words with the slam of her door.

* * * *

"Do you usually come all the way over to this side of town just to get coffee?" Lexi asked Ash, pushing her way through the double doors of Barnes & Noble as they went back outside to get away from the noisy kids waiting for a visiting author. The sun was out, but the air was cool and Lexi curled her hands around the hot paper cup.

"No, I usually go to the Starbucks by school." He came up beside her, the heat from his body fusing with hers, making her pulse skitter. He stepped even closer, near enough their arms brushed. Her blood turned amazingly thick. "I figured you needed a break, so the longer drive over this way, you know?"

Lexi nodded as she took another sip of her mocha latte. He was so easy to be with. No nosy questions, just understanding. Like a friend. Who knew there were guys who weren't sex crazed or controlling?

Ash tipped his head and started walking down the row of shops again. Lexi jogged a couple of steps to catch up then matched her stride to his. They went past a pink and white bath and body shop, then Williams Sonoma.

The setting sun glimmered off the reds and oranges of the tree branches arching across the sidewalk and sparrows hopped around, picking up crumbs left under café tables. Beyond the sidewalk, freshly washed cars pulled in and out of the spaces down the street. Bright-colored delivery trucks rumbled past, wheels humming against the brick-paved streets that led to rows and rows of pretty houses. Typical life in Cherry Grove. Everything just right.

He gave her a nudge with his elbow. "So what was the deal on the phone? You sounded stressed."

There was no point lying. Besides, she needed someone to talk to. Someone who wasn't going to judge her or use the information to talk about her behind her back. "My stupid stepdad, asking stupid questions — as usual."

Ash stopped short, the expression on his face unreadable. "You two don't get along? All the guys on the team think he's okay."

Maybe she'd read him wrong. He wasn't someone she could talk to. Lexi, hoping to keep him from seeing her disgust and resentment, kept walking, swinging her arms and looking around.

"No, really, I want to know." He stopped her, wrapped his free hand behind her back, pulled her snugly to him and guided her forward. "What's the deal?"

That liquid heat came back and she relaxed. After all, he'd never had a stepdad, so how could he know what it was like? This was her chance to explain. "He actually thinks I care about his opinion."

"But you don't care what he thinks, do you?" His voice was light, teasing, and that warmth of understanding encouraged her to look at him.

When she glanced over and spotted his dimple, she grinned. "How'd you guess?"

They paused and moved aside to let a mom wrestling with an overloaded stroller pass. The toddler tagging along behind was squeezing a drink box, making grape juice spurt out of the straw. The purple liquid streamed down her little arm, dripping from her elbow and leaving a drizzly trail on the sidewalk. The mom was trying to capture the girl's hand with one of her own while pushing the stroller with her other. Lexi would've let herself laugh aloud at the awkwardness of it if the poor woman hadn't looked so stressed. Finally the mom scooped the girl up, drippy juice box and all, and carried her toward the parking lot. Her giddy laughter turned to something deeper. She and her mom must've been like that once. The two of them together all the time, her mom looking out for her.

When they started walking again, she shook the thought off, brought herself back to now.

Ash leaned close, practically whispering in her ear, "I sat behind you in zoology last year, remember? You acted like you owned the place, bossing Zoë Weinberg and Sheryl Banter around, making them clean up after every lab." His body vibrated with his low laugh, sending tiny pulses of yummy electricity skittering across her skin. "I don't think you care about anybody's opinion. And you're really, really good at making people do what you say."

Grinning, she bumped him with her hip. "Shut up."

"But I'm right." He lifted his eyebrows and lowered his voice. "Admit it."

"Okay," she said, glancing away because it freaked her out that he actually understood her that well. "It's kind of true."

When she finally got the nerve to look at him again, he was downing the last of his coffee, his throat jerking with the swallows. Once the cup was empty, he pitched it into the trash can at the end of the walkway. It hit the metal rim and thumped to the bottom.

He howled, raising one arm above his head, his whole body shaking as he punched the air. "Who's the man!"

Her body bounced with his, making her snicker. "You're crazy, you know that?"

He howled again, pulled her against him, and she laughed more. For a couple of minutes they walked along, looking at each other and laughing like they were in third grade, except for that awesome tingling inside her skin and the deep thudding in her chest.

After a while Ash broke the silliness with a very brief, light kiss on her cheek, so quick she could have imagined it. Except that warmth came back and she felt protected, secure.

He looked down at her. "Don't worry about Dale, you'll find a way to take care of him."

The giddiness fell away, and she found herself remembering how Dale made her feel. Little. Weak. "You think so?"

"I know it. Losing somebody you don't want to makes you like that. Strong. In control. Capable."

Lexi had never thought of losing her dad that way.

"It makes you different from other people, remember that."

All she remembered was the never-ending pain. "It was a long time after my dad died before I could deal," she said. "At first I didn't even want to talk about it. Think about it. Anything." Remembering about the way Ash had come back to school, only a couple of days after his father died last spring, Lexi added, "But you totally handled it. Everyone was amazed."

"They were?" he said, stiffening with surprise.

She bumped into him, grinning. "Yeah. Of course. That's about the time you really started to stand out."

He lifted an eyebrow, silently asking her to continue.

"It was like you…all of a sudden…" There wasn't a way to say he stopped being a nobody pretty much overnight, so her words hung between them.

He didn't seem to notice her unfinished thought. "I had to grow up all of a sudden," he said. "I guess I wanted…"

They reached the Village Bike shop, the end of the business section, so Ash looped her around and they started back to where they'd left his Mustang. Lexi finished her latte, tossed her cup into the trash can then wrapped her arm behind Ash's back. His muscles were thick and hard. Strong.

"Wanted what?" she asked. "What were you going to say?"

"It sounds lame now, but the whole time growing up, nothing I ever did was good enough for him. So when he died, it was like I wanted to show him how wrong he was." His steps slowed until he stopped moving altogether. She stopped too, waiting silently for him to continue. "I decided I wasn't going to lose anyone ever again and I wasn't ever going to let anyone get in my way."

"Who was in your way?" she asked, amazed that they had that goal in common.

"Doesn't matter anymore. I found a way to take care of it and you're going to help me." Lexi slid him a glance but he was staring ahead, still talking. "Even though he isn't around, I still want my dad to know I'm good enough. I'm going to prove it. It means a lot to me, even though, like I said, I know it sounds lame."

She was going to help him? What did he mean?

"That's not lame," Lexi said, trying to think of a question to keep him talking, anything to get him to explain more.

"Enough about me." His fingers flexed on her waist, bending to match the curves just above her jeans. "You always get what you want. From everyone."

"We'll see," she said, glancing over, wondering what he was getting at, then wondering what he'd say if she asked about Peter.

He started moving again, slowly, as he asked, "You still waiting to hear who Taylor's going to recommend for president?"

She'd have to find a way to get back to that other topic later because this one mattered too. "Yes." She came up behind him and smacked his shoulder with her hand. "And you aren't helping any by not signing for me."

"I'll let the other players— Hey, did I tell you? We have a new guy coming."

They started moving together again. "I don't care about a new guy. I want you."

"I hate that stupid auction." He glanced over at her, a gleam in his eyes. "What if some loser buys me?"

She couldn't tell if he was serious or not. "*I'll* buy you."

Ash halted, his gaze fixed across the street on the small square building tucked behind a row of tall pine trees. "Hey, isn't that Monica Sanders?"

Across the street, Monica was rushing out of the family counseling center, her mom close on her heels, saying something the girl obviously didn't want to hear. Monica stayed a few steps ahead, texting like mad as she hurried across the parking lot.

Lexi's stomach rolled. "What's she doing coming out of there?"

"What do you think?" Ash smirked. "Everyone knows that girl is crazy."

Monica climbed into her mom's white sedan and slammed the door so hard the whole car shook. Her mom lingered in the parking lot, digging her keys out of her purse. "But Monica does everything right. The teachers love her."

"Oh yeah, she's everyone's favorite, that's for sure." He paused, his mouth twisting as he nodded slightly. "But she's messed up."

"I didn't know you knew her."

Ash's face settled into a blank expression, and he shrugged. "I bet there're other people from school that go there."

Lexi watched Monica's mom. At least she cared enough to get her daughter some help. "I never hear anything about anybody getting help like that."

Ash chuckled, low and soft. "Guess they keep each other's secrets."

Lexi's attention shifted to Monica.

"Come on, don't look like that." He nudged her, making her move along with him as he took a few slow steps forward.

Monica's mom pulled the keys out and marched to the driver's side door. Her back was stiff as she yanked open the door and got in. She slammed her door and again the car shook.

Lexi forced a smile.

"Stop thinking about Monica Sanders being screwed in the head. You of all people should be glad."

She turned away from Ash, watching Monica and her mom flash past in Monica's mom's Sebring, their rigid shoulders obvious even from a distance. Once the car was out of sight, she turned back to Ash. "Why do you say that?"

"You aren't friends with her anymore, right?"

"Um, yeah, um, no." She laughed, pretending that none of it mattered while she scrambled to figure out how he knew anything about them being friends at all. They'd been careful, not posting anything, especially pictures, of what they'd been up to.

The expression in Ash's eyes was understanding, not judgmental, and heat from his body wrapped around her, offering comfort and that indescribable electric sizzle. She caught a glimpse of their reflection in one of the shop windows. They looked perfect together — him wearing black leather and her in a pale pink corduroy jacket. She slid out her phone and took a picture of their reflection.

"That's more like it," he said, nudging her with his leg.

"We'll look even better together tomorrow, at Coach's funeral. And everyone will be jealous."

She took a couple more shots. He laughed, grinning as he forced his chest forward, doing what he could to appear bigger.

"Maybe you should make a video of us," he said, making faces and watching his reflection in the window.

Her blood cooled and her stomach turned to stone. Making videos, that was something she never planned to do. Ever again.

She laughed the suggestion off, giggling in a silly way that she knew sounded fake. Thank God he didn't notice because his phone was starting to hum.

Still holding on to her, he pulled it out and hit the screen. The lighthearted humor on his face fell into something close to despair. Maybe it was panic. Worry? With Ash, she was beginning to realize, it was tough to tell what he was thinking. "Oh, God — no." He scrolled down, reading and talking to Lexi at the same time. "Cops found Jon's bike. In the dumpster by the old Westerville diamond." He looked up, his gaze searching. "You know the field I'm talking about?"

Lexi swallowed hard. "Um, yeah. Maybe, I'm not...sure."

Ash tapped his screen, replying without looking up. "The one by the party store with the guy who doesn't check IDs?"

Images of that last night with Monica flickered through Lexi's head, starting with a scene at that exact party store and ending with her and Monica waking up, losing their minds, her putting on Jon's bike gloves and both of them working together to toss his banged-up bike into that very dumpster. "Right. Yeah. I've heard of that place."

"Just heard of it, huh? You never went there to buy?" That causal, easygoing expression came back onto Ash's face. He shoved his cell back into his pocket. "You are sitting with me tomorrow, right?"

"Sure, right," Lexi said, checking her own phone. A text from Jazz, saying her parents weren't going to let her go to the funeral because of the cops finding Jon's bike. No doubt everyone in town knew about the bike by now.

"Meet there a bit before." Ash leaned down and kissed her check. "I want you with me."

Lexi leaned back, sliding into the new connection they'd formed and pretending like his erratic moods weren't weird at all and that she knew nothing about that party store, Jon's bike, the dumpster or Jon.

Chapter Six

Reasons to Be Sorry

Jon's bike getting found stirred everything up, and reporters were chasing down kids, taking pictures and trying to get them to talk. So Saturday afternoon, when Lexi pulled into the parking lot of Willows Chapel and Cemetery, TV cameras, reporters and morbid onlookers milled around in the sharp, cold sunshine. The breezy air snapped with menacing excitement and even though the cops had told everyone to come to them with anything they knew, and keep their mouths shut, kids were standing in clusters, their faces inches from the rolling cameras as they repeated speculation and rumors. In a matter of minutes, the clips would be online, a collage of guesses spoken by pretty but mournful girls and grim-faced teen guys in dark suits. Within hours those bits would be spun together in a series of possible scenarios.

Even though Lexi was supposed to sit with the boosters she waited back, watching the girls merge with the baseball players. The girls clustered around the chapel, a dreary-looking hilltop building made of fat gray stones. The walls of the chapel were grim and dusty-looking, as though the place had been built by medieval druids, or at least designed by video game creators. The contrast with the well-dressed crowd was something else. Any shots the cameramen managed to get of the people inside were going to look great. Most of the boosters were wearing black, even after all the conversation about whether it was really necessary to be traditional. Zoë, always one to do things right, was even wearing black tights and plain black flats. Betty Ann Thompson, who followed behind Zoë, had obviously pulled the charcoal gray suit she was wearing out of her mom's closet—the shoulder pads were so square she looked like SpongeBob. Yet she still had a sexy-secretary look that was turning heads.

Lexi needed to get Monica alone, but the girl was nowhere in sight. Lexi scanned the crowd slowly and carefully. Row after row of stunning Cherry Grove residents, men, women, the high schools kids and even children, all looking fantastic and poised. Another sweep with her gaze and Lexi knew for sure. There was no sign of Taylor either.

One by one the rest of the boosters went in, moving out of the gray day into the gray building. The players followed them, suddenly shoving each other so wildly that the girls had to dodge them to keep from getting knocked down. The guys' nervous laughter cut through the wind, breaking the silence inside the chapel. After Andrea, the last booster to cross through the arched doors, disappeared inside, Lexi wrapped her second-hand Marc Jacobs pea coat tightly around herself to cover her boring, black Ann Taylor dress, and ducked under the low, mostly bare branches of the willow trees.

Three steps later, her cell hummed.

Ash.

You here?

She checked the camera crews, making sure none of them were paying attention to her. They weren't. She went back to her phone but turned away from the crowds still lingering in the parking lot.

Sit in the back row, behind the players.
Where are you?

Be there in a minute, she replied.

Leave together?

Lexi sent 'kk' then started down the walk, tucking her phone into the black bag she'd borrowed from her mom. When she looked back up, a sudden movement caught her eye.

A man, maybe it was a young guy, walking alone toward the chapel door, fighting the autumn wind. His lumpy navy suit hung loose. As he got closer to the chapel doorway, he lifted his head, scanning, searching for something — someone. Lexi couldn't see his face, but something about him was familiar. Maybe it was the way he walked? Or his silhouette?

With his rumpled suit and messed-up hair, he didn't look like a teacher. Maybe a sub?

Somebody working for the media, ready to catch the latest rumor about Jon?

Lexi slowed, watching him as she, too, headed for the door.

He wasn't part of the press. Not dressed that way.

Maybe a coach from one of the other schools?

Whoever he was, something about him gave Lexi the creeps. The way he kept pulling his collar over his face and tugging on his suit—ick. Inside, he merged with the crowd, and she quickly lost track of him.

Finally Lexi went in, slid in next to Troy Donaldson. He looked over and winked, then whispered, "You make an awesome Goth chick."

She rolled her eyes but still smiled. "Gee. Thanks."

"Hey, Ash wanted me to tell you he has to say some stuff as part of the memorial, but he'll be back here as soon as he's done."

"Thanks." Lexi spotted Ash in the front row with Mrs. Archer, patting her back and telling her something. She was leaning against him, accepting the support of his shoulder as she nodded slowly.

The boosters were about five rows back from Ash and the others up front. Betty Ann was putting on even more lip gloss, and Zoë was reading the remembrance card. Taylor and Monica had appeared out of nowhere and now sat with their heads together, looking like best friends. A bad sign. Really bad. And how was Lexi going to talk to Monica if Taylor was hovering nearby?

Monica glanced over and caught Lexi's eye, scowled and looked down. Seconds later Lexi's cell hummed.

Stop staring.

Lexi's fingers hovered over the screen, but she put her phone back in her bag, turned around and stared ahead.

The service started with soft organ music meant to soothe, but it really only punctuated the fact that somebody was dead. The sound echoed off the stone walls and vibrated in the air. Nobody seated in the rows moved. The pastor, looking like he was used to things like old guys everybody loved and respected dying for no reason, settled behind the podium and clipped on a wireless mic. He started the service by talking about how God "has plans for each and everyone one of us, but we don't get to know what they are."

No kidding about that second part.

After the pastor finished with the opening remarks, Ash got up and stood between the two huge bouquets of bright white lilies, strong and steady in his charcoal gray suit. His eyes calm. Focused. Like he was staring down a batter, daring him to get a hit. He spoke for a few minutes, saying the stuff Lexi expected to hear. Coach had been a great man, believed in his players and supported them but made them work hard, pushed them to do more than they thought they could. When he finished, he paused for a few seconds, looking out at the crowd, his expression calm.

Other people, maybe other coaches or players from years ago, talked too. They all mentioned Coach Filpot's solid work ethic and his way of making people keep going even when they didn't want to. Their comments, too, were probably the normal thing to expect, but for Lexi it was like watching a bad cartoon. Stiff, fake and unpleasant.

When the pastor planted himself between the lilies and asked the gathering to bow their heads for a final prayer, Ash caught Lexi's eye and smiled. It was a soft, subtle smile meant just for her. Her heart thumped, pushing blood through her veins. She smiled back.

After the prayer, while people were looking up, getting ready for the last part of the service, Ash tiptoed down the aisle and slid in next to Lexi. He nudged her shoulder with his and whispered, "Hi. Can't leave with you, sorry. Mrs. Archer wants me to go get Peter and bring him to the Filpots'." Ash smirked and said softly into her ear, "He's in big trouble."

The pastor concluded the service and announced it was time to go to the burial site.

Leaning back, Ash took Lexi's hand and added, "Come on, let's go out to the grave."

A group of guys, some players and some probably relatives, carried the coffin down the center aisle of the chapel.

Outside, it was a grim but picturesque affair. A cough, a sniffle, some black-haired kid complaining about his tight shoes. Bright autumn trees catching the occasional ray of sunlight, all the while tossing dazzling leaves into the wind, giving the place an air of freedom and the scent of nature. There was a stone-solid quiet as the procession stepped through the freshly cut grass, trudging along. The setting at the gravesite was carefully arranged. A green carpet of fake grass had been stretched over the hole in the ground, and a circle of yellow and white bouquets surrounded the area. A small table covered with long-stemmed yellow roses stood off to the side.

But it wasn't as idealistic as it appeared. Off in the distance, a burly guy steadying a TV camera on his shoulder swept to the side of the parking lot, probably using the best lens he had to catch the grief of Coach's family — and a few shots of Taylor, who was right in the middle of everything, looking simultaneously sad and vibrant.

Pivoting, Lexi scanned the crowd for the shabby guy, but he'd vanished. Must have gotten what he came for. Whatever it was.

No Monica either.

The pastor stopped at Coach's final resting place, a spot near a cluster of precisely trimmed pines. One by one people circled and stood, hands clutched together, crammed in pockets, or, like Lexi's and Ash's, linked. Beside her Ash was confident, in control, sexy and solid all at the same time. He looked like he could step right onto polo.com. Except for the very genuine grief pulling on his mouth. It occurred to Lexi, maybe this was what he'd been talking about the day before, when he'd said she was going to help him with something.

The pastor began the graveside service by talking about faith, but his words were quickly drowned out by the wails of the complaining kid as his mom pulled him from the crowd. As the kid's whining faded, the pastor's words grew louder, and Lexi listened while half wondering what exactly was going on in Cherry Hill. The faces of the crowd stayed emotionless, denying that bad things happened. But that obviously wasn't the case.

The graveside portion of the ceremony was much shorter and soon the crowd was breaking up, the chatter and tears growing louder as people moved away, heading up and over the hill. Before leaving the graveside, Lexi accepted one of the yellow roses Taylor had brought for the boosters. She tossed it onto the casket, then she and Ash melted into the group oozing across the cemetery grounds toward the parking lot.

Lexi scanned the lot. No sign of Monica — her car wasn't even there.

"Lexi! Ash! Wait up!"

Zoë Weinberg.

The chubby girl huffed up, her breath coming in little train engine puffs. Red blotches covered her cheeks, and even though she was sort of smiling, her mouth was quivering, making her look as though she was going to burst into tears. "You guys weren't around when I passed out the flyers. I'm having people over."

"You're having a party?" Lexi asked, hearing her shock.

"But it's just for us, you know, kids from Cherry Grove, so don't post anything about it." She frowned and waved her hand to the camera crews and news vans still swarming at the main entrance of the lot. "We don't want them showing up."

"That's the truth," Ash said. "They're ruining everything."

"The party was my mom's idea. A wake. Without parents and all that, so we'll be able to talk, spend time together." Zoë pulled a flyer from her Burberry bag, holding it out with a jangle of bright metal bangles. "It's tonight at seven. Can you come?"

It was weird, having a party after a funeral, but it seemed like a good idea, everyone being together without parents or cops or counselors or media. Lexi glanced at Ash. He nodded, so she said, "Sure, of course. Thanks."

Zoë, always the one concerned about making sure everyone had a good time, started chattering about food. "I could do a simple cheese and cracker layout or maybe call the caterers for something more, well, not festive but, you know, nicer."

"You're great at this stuff, Zoë," Ash said, leaning over to smile at Zoë.

"Ash is right," Lexi added. "Whatever you decide will be perfect." But what she was really thinking was that the guys would eat whatever food was sitting out regardless of what it was or even looked like, and most of the girls weren't going to touch it.

"Thanks. You guys are always so great, not like some of the other people around here. What about the music? Stuff like Radiohead? Or Flo Rida? Maybe Spaz could make a mix? Or—"

"Hey," Ash cut in. "Okay if I invite Zeke? He didn't know Coach, but he just moved here, so it'd be good if he could meet people. Show support."

"Sure, that's a great idea." Zoë slowed to a stop. "That kind of sucks that he moved here in the middle of all this." Then she waved goodbye and puffed off, her lumpy jacket making her look like a little bear as she dodged between the cars backing out and rambled toward her burgundy Volvo wagon.

Lexi nudged Ash. "Who's Zeke?"

He took her hand. "A catcher."

"You know him from baseball?" Lexi asked, looking for Monica but seeing only clusters of kids talking into cameras again. The media crews were blocking the end of the parking lot, and some guy in a mud-spattered Honda Fit was leaning out the window, yelling as he honked the car's feeble horn.

"Yeah, sort of. We were at camp together a couple times, way back when we were kids." His voice lowered as he added, "Not that he remembers it, though."

"You guys are friends now?" she asked, having to raise hers to speak over another car horn and the rumble of a couple pickup trucks racing off in the opposite direction, going to the far end of the lot where they could get out without having to weave through the media.

The chaos in the parking lot caught Ash's attention. He looked over and pointed. "The cops finding Jon's bike really doesn't change anything. He's still gone and nobody knows why. Then coach dies. It's making everyone act weird. Stressed."

Lexi pressed her lips together, too afraid to say anything. One thought spoken would lead to another, and another, then who knew what she'd say.

Ash's gaze circled her face, finally stopping on her eyes. "Sorry. Didn't mean to freak you out." Turning his back on the scene, putting it between them, he took her other hand and said, "Zeke needs friends. He had some trouble at his old school, some scene that wasn't his fault. His family moved here to get away from all the drama." Ash let go of her hands and stepped back. "Speaking of trouble, I better go get Peter."

He gave her a quick kiss on the cheek then, without even a goodbye, he headed to his car, shoulders swaying beneath the dark suit. Lexi watched him walk away, heat and nervous energy sizzling in her blood.

If only it could all just go away. Then she and Ash could spend time getting to know each other instead of talking about everyone else. Lexi's phone hummed. She dug it out and smiled at the message. Jazz inviting her over because her parents were gone for a couple of hours. A break from all the drama was just what she needed and — bonus — going to Jazz's gave her somewhere to go for a while instead of home. She sent back a text telling her about Zoë's party and saying she'd be over in a few. As she drove toward the back entrance of the parking lot, she finally saw Monica, perched on the hood of Troy's restored black Chevelle. The outfielder was angled over her — she was pulling on the collar of his brown leather car coat, her dark hair shimmering in the clear autumn sunlight.

Lexi slowed. Monica's face was tight, though — anxious. Desperate? Maybe things weren't so perfect with her and Taylor after all. Or maybe she was worried about the bike too.

Tonight, at Zoë's, she and Monica were definitely going to talk.

Chapter Seven

More Hot Water

Later that night, after dinner, Lexi sat on her bed, staring into her closet. Wearing something sexy to Zoë's party didn't seem right—it was a wake, after all. A celebration of death. Kind of weird, for sure. But that didn't mean she had to look boring, did it?

The skimpy Niki Smith dress she'd found at the resale shop was out, even though it made her butt look rounder. Ditto the Lucky Brand jeans. Her short black miniskirt and low-cut peasant top seemed decent enough, but would still get Ash's attention. To avoid Dale's usual string of nosy questions, and prevent him from giving her that disgusting look, she tucked them into her backpack. She'd ask Jazz to stop somewhere on the way to Zoë's so she could change and put her makeup on. Anything to avoid dealing with the loser. In order to deal with Monica she needed to be calm and focused.

But the ploy didn't do her any good. Dale strolled into her room as she was scooping up her makeup and hair spray. He didn't even have the decency to knock. Her throat tightened as he lowered his dirty self into the delicate chair at her desk. As always, the smell of burnt metal floated around him, drifting like a cloud around until it reached her.

Pointing his callused fingers to her backpack, he asked, "Where're you off to? What's in the pack?"

"School stuff," she replied, disregarding his first question and praying he would get a clue and get the hell out of her room.

Instead, he sat there looking around, scrutinizing her things as though he'd be able to detect some sort of misbehavior or dark secret. Finding nothing, he turned his attention to the photos on her desk, his gaze creeping across each bright face before turning back to add, "Seems like you're gone a lot. Don't you realize how that upsets your mother?"

The nasty smell, the disgusting grease stains on his blue work pants, even his voice made her nauseated. Resentful.

Angry.

"You don't have to pretend to care about me," she said, squeezing the queasiness out of her voice but letting the emotions through. "I don't care about you." It felt good to say it aloud. "Go ahead," she added, gaining strength, "leave again. Please."

He set his palms on his knobby knees and leaned forward. "Your mom doesn't want me to go."

Lexi winced at the truth of it.

Yes, he knew which lever to yank, but she wasn't going to let him win. "Mom doesn't know what she wants. The way you take advantage of her, she probably never will."

He cast aside her accusations with a bony shrug. "I need to talk to you 'bout the team."

She grabbed her bag then turned her back to him as she stuffed her strappy heels into it. "I've got to get ready," she said, even though she already had everything she needed. "So could you please…" She pointed to the door.

Of course he stayed seated, defiling her room with his presence. "I heard about the new kid, Zeke, the catcher, and since you're dating Ash—"

She spun around, scoffing. "You've got to be kidding, acting like you're part of what goes on around here."

"You don't get it, do you?" he murmured, looking at one of the photos he'd picked up from her desk. "Why do you think I came back?"

"Because you ran out of money or you got tired of doing your own laundry." She threw one hand in the air. "How should I know?" Swinging her backpack over her shoulder, she stepped toward the door. "I'm going out front to watch for Jasmine and—"

"Hold it." Gently, he set the photo down, got up, and planted himself in the middle of the room, closer to her. "I'm keeping my eye on you. You need someone to watch out for you, Lexi. You aren't good at taking care of yourself."

Clutching the strap of her backpack, she ground her words out. "I don't need you. And I don't want you."

"The night I came home, your mom and I straightened your room up, like before, when you were still my Lexi-girl. You do need me." He stalked toward her, adding softly, "You're the reason I came back."

Electrified by anger, she shied away, but he blocked her exit and lifted his rough hands, reaching for her with his horrible grubby fingers.

One quick step and his arms could surround her.

Lexi lunged past him, taking the stairs two at a time. She'd be leaving without saying goodbye to her mom. Thank God Jasmine's yellow bug was stopping at the curb just as she slammed the front door.

Lexi ran to the curb, jerked open the door and threw herself into the car. Seconds later she had her seatbelt clicked and her stuff on the floor between her feet.

Eyeing Lexi's backpack, Jasmine asked, "Need me to stop at Mickey D's again?"

"Yeah. Thanks."

Jasmine's gaze circled Lexi's face just before she put the car in drive. "Dale?"

Half expecting to see the loser running after them, Lexi twisted to check out the back window. "I tried to avoid him, but he came in my room and started acting weird, saying he wanted to talk about the team. Then he asked about Ash's friend Zeke."

"Who's Zeke?"

"A guy who just moved here. Plays baseball, I guess."

Jazz reached the end of Lexi's block and turned. "Why is Dale asking about him?"

"I don't know. Peter was talking about him too." Right before he ditched her, jerk that he was. "He said he played in the Little League World Series, so I guess he's a big deal. Like it even matters?" Lexi stared at her phone, her thoughts zipping between horrible Dale and getting her head ready to talk to self-serving Monica.

"You'd think people would be more worried about Jon instead of a season that isn't going to start for months."

Lexi ran her thumb along the side of her cell, considering. "Have you heard anything more about that? I mean, besides them finding Jon's bike?"

"No." Jazz hit her blinker and eased around a corner, heading toward the McDonald's down the street from the school. "Some kids are saying that the cops are starting to get cell records and Facebook posts."

Lexi's fingers stiffened. "Cell records?"

"Yeah, they can get old texts too, I guess."

Crap. Lexi threw her phone into her bag.

Jazz chuckled, glancing at Lexi's bag. "What, you never thought about that? Worried Dale might start getting your texts? Track you? I don't think even my parents would stoop that low. I hope not anyway. But if they do find out about my sneaking out, who the hell knows what they'll do."

"They just want you to be safe." Lexi forced a smile. "Dale alone is way worse than both your parents put together."

Jazz curled her lip. "He is such a freak."

Lexi leaned back and watched the rows of white houses near the school flash past. The gray clouds would've looked gloomy if it weren't for the bright leaves gleaming from the branches of the trees. "He was saying he came back home because of me. What does that even mean?"

"I have no idea. That's more than his usual jerkishness," Jazz replied, casting her a quick, sympathetic glance. "You don't think he meant it like that?"

"No, even he isn't *that* bad."

"Did you say anything to your mom?"

"Nah. She's so happy he's back, she'd never listen." Trying to get her mom to understand how much she hated Dale was impossible, but she intended to keep on doing it. "Right now I just want to forget about him and his disgusting crap."

Jazz pulled into the Mickey D's parking lot. The place was circled by minivans and SUVs and dotted with people coming and going. "I'm all for forgetting about that. Hurry up and go change."

Lexi grabbed her stuff from the back seat then slid out. Three steps later, unable to control herself, she texted Monica, but only a simple question—

You going to be at Zoë's?

She'd better be. Or Lexi was going to show up on her doorstep.

* * * *

As they got closer to Zoë's house, the sides of the street were more and more crowded with cars and groups of kids. Some kids were still wearing their clothes from the funeral, but most, like Lexi and Jazz, had changed into something subdued but decent. Music from car radios rolled through the night air, Katy Perry, Pitbull and that goofy *Sweet Caroline* song by Neil Diamond, all blended together.

Jazz slowed and pointed to the girls with the Neil Diamond coming from a gray Volvo. The three of them leaned against the back of the car, passing a water bottle around and singing at the top of their lungs. "It doesn't sound good," she said. "And in about thirty minutes, it isn't going to look good either."

"No doubt." One of the girls was already having trouble standing. Another one was scooping up bunches of leaves and tossing them on herself, laughing as she sang. Lexi turned away. Thank God those days were over for her.

Jazz cruised down a bit farther. She found a spot and backed in. "Hey, all right with you if I go find Alan?"

"You guys are still okay, right?"

"Yeah. Ever since they found Jon's bike he's been crazy, but he's not taking it out on me anymore."

"Of course I don't mind." Lexi followed her friend up the glossy stone walkway to the ridiculously long front porch lined with pots so giant each one held nearly a whole garden of flowers. Swinging around one of the fat white pillars, she said, "I'm trying to run into Ash anyway."

And find Monica.

Jazz lifted her perfectly arched brows. "Still trying to get Ash to sign?"

Lexi spun around the pillar again, circling in time to the music blaring from inside the house. "It started out that way, but I'm thinking we've got more going on now."

"Yeah? He seems…" Jazz stalled, obviously searching for the right word.

"Different," Lexi finished easily. "Not like all the other guys."

"I guess that's what I was thinking," Jazz replied, putting her hand on the huge lion head door knocker, banging hard against the door.

"Nobody is going to hear that." Lexi reached past her, opened the door with a silly flourish, and stepped onto the sleek parquet floor. "Tell Alan I said hey," she called over her shoulder.

"Sure thing," Jazz said, heading to the right.

Lexi turned left, passed through a hall and headed to the kitchen. Having a drink of something in her hands was a trick she'd learned to keep people from shoving beers on her. A trick she'd learned months too late, but she couldn't go back in time and change what she'd done.

If only.

Shortie and Spaz, the only two people in the room, leaned over the wide, center-room island, a giant collection of gleaming copper pots hanging over their heads.

"Hey, Lexi," they said in unison, their heads bobbing in sync. The music from the other end of the house was so loud they had to raise their voices.

"Hey," she called back as she pulled a bottle of water from the refrigerator. She took a sip then scooted over to where they sat bouncing quarters into their half-full glasses of orange pop. "I didn't know people still played quarters."

"It's retro," said Spaz, stretching the words out slowly.

"Um, okay," she replied, smiling at his silliness. "But aren't you supposed to do that with beer?"

"Not me and my boy, we don't mess with that." Spaz did some kind of thing with his hand, like he was having a seizure or something. "We athletes, guurrl."

Lexi laughed.

"Besides," Shortie added, rolling a coin off his nose, "my dad would kill me, take me off the team."

They actually took baseball seriously?

She eyed them with new respect, until Spaz started giggling at Shortie's disgusting belch.

"Hey, Lexi, Monica's looking for you, by the way," Spaz said, once he got control of himself.

"She's back in the media room," Shorty added, tapping a quarter on the table. His gaze locked on his opponent, he added, "Good luck finding her, though. Everybody in Cherry Grove is crammed into there."

"Hey," Shortie complained, lifting his glass. "Stop that tapping, you loser, you're driving me to drink!" He took a huge gulp and burped again.

Spaz whipped a quarter at him.

"You two have fun with that." Lexi went down the hall, crossing through the dimly lit living room. Stray couples huddled in dark corners, some making out, others just getting ready to. She tried to make sure Ash wasn't among them, but it was impossible without being totally rude, so she gave up and kept walking.

Probably better to find Monica first. Deal with her, then spend the rest of her night with Ash.

Spaz and Shortie were right. The back room was jammed. It was so packed she had to edge her way in, pressing against guys she wouldn't let near her if they paid her and pushing aside the freshmen girls trying to get their attention. Like all the houses in this section of town, the house was huge and designed for entertaining. Heavy bass shook the floor and an immense flat screen filled the back wall. *Frozen* was playing, with the sound off. Dance music beat from ceiling-mounted speakers, bodies bounced, rave lighting flickered a spectrum of neon, and a couple people had glow sticks. As she wove her way through the mass of bodies, a girl sitting on some guy's shoulders, her arms waving like snakes, yelled at Lexi. She waved back, still searching, but no Monica.

Zoë rushed over, her round body stuffed into a lumpy green cable sweater and some kind of not-quite-right tan dress pants. "Come get something to eat," she yelled over the thumping, pulling Lexi to the lacquered bar that ran the length of the side wall. It was overloaded with dishes of food, trays of cheese, bags of chips and half-empty beer cups. So much for the caterer.

At Zoë's insistence, Lexi climbed onto one of the tall barstools and checked out the huge blue fish mounted above shelves that were completely covered with liquor bottles. Giant lures, extra thick poles and other oversized fishing stuff was everywhere. There was even a huge net hanging from the ceiling.

The song switched to a slow one by Lily Allen and sections of the mob broke apart, others clung together, swaying and singing along. Zoë reached between the bodies and pulled out a guy wearing a turtleneck and dark jeans.

"Hey, Lexi." His deep voice broke through the music.

Lexi reeled, reaching for the edge of the bar to steady herself, clutching it with shaking fingers. Her hearted stalled then thumped. "Hey." She faked a relaxed smile and pretended to be okay. But the fact was, those rowdy, destructive summer months with Monica were colliding with the present.

Zoë beamed. "Oh, you two already know each other! Perfect!"

"You look awesome. I like that skirt," he said, fingering the hem with quick fingers, touching her like it was no big thing.

Of course he had touched her that way before, so it wasn't. To him, anyway.

"Hey there." Lexi's voice got lost in the noise, but her eyes couldn't stop staring at 'Z'. Smooth skin, long-lashed, bright green eyes and gorgeous chiseled features. A regular hottie in all the ways that mattered.

Guess that was why she and Monica had kept going back to that convenience store. That, and that he'd sold them whatever they'd wanted to buy. And gone along with whatever they'd wanted to do.

Obviously unaware of Lexi's anguish, Zoë's round face lit up with satisfaction. "So, you two are all set," she said, then disappeared among the bodies.

"Dance with me." Zeke snaked his long arm around Lexi's waist and leaned in, his mouth so close to her neck she could feel his lips move across her skin. "It'll give you something to do until you get that look off your face." He hauled her into the sweaty, vibrating mob.

Zeke tugged her closer, pulling her snugly to his muscular chest then dropping his hand to the top of her butt. At least he wasn't squeezing her ass right there in front of everyone. Lexi glanced around, looking for Ash. Praying he wasn't watching.

Where is that damn Monica?

"Aren't you going to try to get me to sign for that auction thing?" he asked, rubbing against her.

Lexi tried to push him away, but his grip was firm. Shoving him away would cause a scene and that definitely wasn't what she wanted. "I wasn't expecting to see you," she said, loudly enough for him to hear. "Pretty much ever again."

He laughed into her ear. His warm breath made a shiver scurry down her spine. "Neither was Monica. You should have seen the look on her face when that Zoë girl introduced us."

"Monica? Why would she care? She doesn't care about anything."

Zeke loosened his grip enough to look down at her, his green eyes flashing. "You don't know?" He touched her face and kept his mouth near when he said, "I thought you two shared everything."

"Know what?" Lexi bumped into some girl then stumbled. Zeke swept her away from the girl and steadied her. "And we aren't friends anymore."

His crooked smile inches from her mouth, he said, "Then you really want to know what I know." Zeke nuzzled her neck, running his lips up and down her throat then whispering, "Meet me in the hot tub. If things go right, I'll tell you."

Not giving her a chance to say no, he pressed his finger to her lips. "I'll shut the door to the porch. Knock four times, so I'll know it's you." With that, he let go and shouldered through the throng.

The music hyped and kids howled, guys laughing as they raised their fists. Guys and girls started hopping, jumping to the wild, steady pounding. Lexi stepped back, toward the doorway then through the hall, away from the heat and noise. Even more kids had arrived, making it difficult to walk quickly. She moved as fast as she could, glancing side to side as she headed back the way she'd come.

No Ash. But Monica was headed straight for her, face tight.

"You need to stay away from Ash," she said, taking hold of Lexi's arms and forcing her into a small study off the living room.

"What?" Lexi grabbed at Monica's fingers as the girl dragged her deeper into the room.

"What the hell is your problem?" she asked, letting go of Lexi to move back to close the French door. "Just listen to me, okay?" she said.

Lexi scoffed. "Why should I listen to anything you say?"

"I've been totally honest with you. I told you about Jon, right?" She checked over her shoulder, looking through the glass door, then said, "It's not like I'm pretending nothing happened."

The memory of throwing Jon's bike in the dumpster was followed by images of TV crews interviewing kids, and all those thoughts of 'what if' filled Lexi's mind. And what had Zeke been getting at? He knew something about Monica that she didn't? "Yeah, that's fine and all, but—" She rushed forward then came at the other girl more slowly. "I have some questions I want answered about—"

"I got another text from Jon last night. He's fine. So keep your mouth shut." When Lexi didn't back off, Monica continued, "Look, even if he was gone—which he isn't—we don't really know anything."

This time Lexi grabbed Monica's arm and pulled her close. She looked up and saw each of the girl's delicate lashes and the sparkle of her gold eyeliner. So pretty. So bad. "We woke up with his bike on the hood of your car."

"But he wasn't with it."

Lexi squeezed her fingers, feeling Monica's soft flesh, smelling the Chanel No. 5 she always wore. "What if—?"

"Shut up," Monica said, tugging her arm away with a quick jerk. "There is no what if so stop thinking about it. And get it through your head that nobody cares that we spent the whole summer getting wasted."

She was right about that, but not about other things they'd done. "What we did was a felony, Monica. I looked it up. If we get caught—"

For the first time ever, Monica's face went blank, the ever-present sweet pinkness in her cheeks gone. "I know that. I looked it up too. But stop stressing because it's getting taken care of. I'm taking care of it." The nastiness came back, and a ruddy red flush brightened her face. "Besides, we'd just get lawyers if we had to."

Maybe that was true for Monica—her parents could afford the best and she didn't need scholarships and financial aid to get the hell out of Cherry Grove. But Lexi lived in a different world, one where girls who did nasty tricks had to pay for what they'd done. If the cops found out what had gone on at the Westerville party store Lexi was going to be stuck in Cherry Grove, living at home and going to Westerville Community College. If she didn't end up in jail.

"And listen to me about Ash. Stay away from him."

"Whatever, Monica. I'm so going to listen to you." Lexi started to back away, but stopped. "By the way, what's up with Zeke? What does he know about you?"

"Stay away from him, too."

"Yeah, right. I'll totally do that." Lexi pushed past Monica to get out of the room. She opened the door and stepped around a couple of kids dancing in the hall.

Zoë, always the perfect hostess, kept extra bathing suits in the guest bathroom by the kitchen, so Lexi looped through the living room, which was starting to look like a casting call for a porn video, then went in the opposite direction of the media room.

Nothing about the Weinbergs' house was small, so the bathroom was more of a sitting room with a bathroom attached. Everything in there was either a cheery blue or white, including the cozy plaid couch. If things were different, she might have taken a minute to appreciate the cute flower-shaped soaps and fine blue linen towels embroidered with delicate white flowers.

Zeke wasn't going to get what he wanted from Lexi, but from what she knew about him, he'd take his disappointment in stride. He'd certainly been disappointed by her in the past. So one more time wasn't going to matter. Besides, with his gorgeous body and man-beautiful face, he wouldn't have to look long until he found a girl willing to do what she wasn't.

Lexi dug through the basket. No surprise, there were suits of all sizes and colors. She slipped into a black Calvin Klein one-piece, tucked her thong into her shoes, which she left behind the couch, then put her clothes back on over her suit. No way was she walking past all those horny guys wearing only a swimsuit. When she went by the kitchen, Spaz and Shortie were still posted up at the table, playing quarters.

"Don't you guys get it?" Pointing to the hall, she added, "The actual party is down there."

"Yeah, we thought about going down there and eating all Zoë's food, but then we wouldn't get to talk to all the hot babes coming out of the bathroom." Shortie giggled, all high-pitched and snorting.

Spaz fell apart, laughing, spilling the entire contents of the cup in his hand. It swirled across the island top then dripped orange fizz onto the tile floor. Shorty reached over to grab a stack of paper napkins. He tossed some across the mess then threw some at Spaz. "On your knees, loser, get to work."

Lexi stepped over the bright stream of pop streaming across the floor, grabbed two cans of Coke from the fridge, then went to get the dirt on Monica from Zeke.

The hot tub was in a walled garden room on the Weinbergs' wraparound deck, hidden from view by a screen of huge, wide-leafed tropical plants. Thank God most of the kids didn't even know it was there, so nobody was around to see her meeting up with Zeke. The volume of the music and the heat from the crowd had both increased, making the hall even harder to get through.

She knocked four times. Nothing.

She rapped on the door again, waited, listened, but still nothing. *Jerk.* She didn't have time for games.

She curled her fingers around the brass door handle. It opened.

Expecting to find Zeke with his back against the tiles and a cocky grin on his perfect mouth, she straightened and eased the door all the way open. Zeke, still dressed and still dry, was flattened against the wall, his face a mask of white shock.

"I found, he—I—" he said, pointing at the hot tub, where Peter Archer's limp body floated, half in, half out of the hissing bubbles. His mouth was wide open and filled with water.

Liquid and heavy, Lexi stumbled back, the cans smacking onto the floor, rolling over the tile. One popped open, hissed brown fizz, spitting Coke over the pristine white tile floor. She backed out of the room. Waves of steam followed her out to the hall, moisture skimming over her face. She limped on wobbly legs, shoving at people as she went.

She got to the end of the hall and stopped. Maybe he wasn't actually dead.

Lexi braced herself as she lurched back to the deck. She slipped back through the door and looked at Zeke. "Pull him out."

Zeke stared back at her, his face a blank slate.

"Pull him out," she said again, this time with more grit.

He moved forward, knelt at the edge of the steaming hot tub and looked up at her. She nodded. He reached in and grabbed Peter, turned him over. Peter's body flipped, water splashing onto the floor as Zeke struggled to pull him out. After three tugs he moaned, let go, rolled back and threw up beside a potted tree.

Lexi's arms and legs sagged, soft and unwilling, as she dropped against the wall, collapsing into a heap. The bitter scent of Zeke's vomit filled the air, making her own stomach heave. She crawled out of the room, into the hall, and sat. When she looked up, *he* was there.

Relief flooded through her. "Ash," she murmured. He pulled her up, pressing her back against the wall and steadying her with his warm hands.

"What's wrong?"

Even as she choked out the words, she hardly believed them herself. "Peter—he's dead. In the hot tub. Just floating. Not moving. Dead. And Zeke—he—"

"No, Lexi"—he placed one palm on each side of her, protecting her—"Peter's not dead. He must've passed out. You know how he is, always has to be the dude who drinks the most."

She blinked away the picture of Peter's floating body. But it came right back.

Her head rolled to the side, her vision filled with bodies—moving slowly down the hall, standing still, writhing, and surrounding them all was the constant boom and bass of the music echoing its way from the media room. She looked back to Ash.

"Come on." He took her out of the hall, set her on one of the soft, brown leather chairs in the dark living room. When one of the couples broke apart and asked what was wrong, Lexi realized she'd been sobbing softly. Instead of answering, she just stared ahead.

"Nothing's wrong," Ash said to the couple. They shrugged and turned back to each other, their lips connecting as their arms wrapped around each other. Ash let go of Lexi and stepped back. "Stay here," he said, then left her there, in the dark.

Alone.

She closed her eyes, sank deeper into the chair, waited.

But when Ash came back, he didn't stop for her. He jogged past, tapping his cell as he pushed his way down the hall to the media room. Troy leaped up from one of the dark corners and took off after him.

The music stopped, kids rushed past, anxious to face death waiting for them on the deck. Guys started shouting. Zoë appeared out of nowhere, crying, her round face turning red.

Lexi's breath hitched in her throat, her vision turned hazy.

"Troy. Don't let Zeke leave," someone shouted. "The cops have to do that CSI stuff."

Shrill screams pierced Lexi's ears. She gasped for air, struggling to get a grip on herself. Then everything went dark.

Chapter Eight

Too Late to Be Sorry?

Thin, misty fog hugged Ash's Mustang as it rolled down Grove Avenue. Traffic lights passed overhead like hazy neon stars, guiding the way to the cop station. They'd left the radio off, so the hum of the engine as he shifted through the gears was the only sound as the houses blurred past. They'd left the party only minutes ago, but Lexi's sense of time was warped.

The scenes frozen in her mind could have been from days or months ago, or even something that she'd imagined. Peter's angular body spread across the floor, his handsome face bobbing in the water. Zeke's white, emotionless face as he puked. Coke oozing across the tiles like fizzing blood.

The cops were going to ask questions. She scrambled to put the pieces of the night together, like where she'd been before going out to the Weinbergs' garden room, how long she and Zeke had been apart. How long she'd been with Monica. What they'd talked about.

A fresh roll of fear crashed through Lexi.

Monica.

That conversation couldn't be part of her story.

Then a question. What had Zeke been ready to tell her? Did Monica have a secret? Tapping into her thoughts, Ash said, "The detective's going to want to know everything. You remember what happened?"

"I'm trying, but it's all jumbled together." She snuggled closer, wanting his strength and desperately wishing the part with Monica hadn't happened. "The only thing that's clear is you picking me up."

Keeping his eyes on the road, Ash nodded.

A whisper of guilt slid across her shoulders. She should call her mom, tell her where she was headed. Dale or no Dale, her mom would want to know.

Holding in a sigh, she dug out her phone.

Ash glanced over, eyeing her phone. "Who're you calling?"

"My mom." She tapped the screen and it blinked, casting a faint glow across Ash's face.

"There's nothing she can do." He looked back to the road. "Don't you think you'll just freak her out?" When Lexi's fingers wavered above the screen, he added, "I didn't call mine. She'll just ask a bunch of questions you can't answer."

Her mom would take that a step further and pull Dale into the mix. Within seconds, he'd have her convinced that the whole thing was Lexi's fault, like she was some sort of demon child. Her mom would start crying. That drama was the last thing she needed.

"You're right." Lexi tossed her phone back into her bag, closed it and rested her arms on top.

With an easy bend of his wrist and a smooth downshift, Ash turned right onto Pine, and she settled into his protective silence.

Soon he was easing into a spot in the nearly empty station lot. The pale, ghostly gleam of the spotlights flickered through the darkness. He lumbered out, strode through that bleak light to come around and open the door on her side, but she stalled as a new question popped up in her mind.

Did she have to tell the cops that the last time she'd seen Peter was when he'd ditched her at the movies? That was two nights ago so maybe not. Telling them that would lead to telling the whole story and that would get Jazz into serious trouble. And it wasn't like telling would bring Peter back to life, anyway.

"Come on," he said. "Let's get it over with."

She took Ash's outstretched hand, let him pull her from the car, and they went through the automatic doors.

A gray-haired, uniformed cop lingered behind the long front desk, flipping through papers and glancing at the monitors in front of him. As they moved forward, he watched them with watery eyes, his mouth pulling down into a frown. His badge caught the fluorescent light, sending a flash of warning to everyone around.

Ash went straight up, pressed himself against the counter. "We were at the party. We need to speak to someone. Right away."

"Name?" the cop asked, looking bored as he reached for a clipboard stacked with forms.

Ash tipped his head. "This is Lexi Welks, she found the guy in the hot tub."

The officer paused, took a longer look at them, then pointed to a row of chairs against the wall, his expression still flat. "Sit over there. No talking. No phones."

The man stepped sideways, keeping one wary eye on them, and reached for a phone. After they dropped into some seats he made a call, saying little, waiting a lot. As each minute passed, Lexi's heart beat faster even though a strange weariness settled over her. The images of the night began to blend together. How could it be so quiet? A sixteen-year-old kid was dead, and it was like nothing had happened.

Time passed. If only she could just go home, crawl into bed and pull the covers over her. Beside her, Ash shifted in his chair, crossing and uncrossing his legs. She waited for him to look over at her but his gaze stayed forward, focused on a group of potted plants circling a trash can. A rack of magazines, mostly about sports cars and outdoor sports, hung beside it.

The time that passed could've been minutes or hours. Lexi's mind went blank, her body numb. It was as though she simply couldn't think about what had happened any longer. She leaned over, put her head on Ash's shoulder. He was her hook to reality, and she let her thoughts of the night gently fade until the officer appeared in front of them and barked, "Come with me, both of you."

Ash took Lexi's hand and squeezed it as they got up to follow the cop down a short hallway, away from the cozy paneling in the reception area to the back of the station. The man paused at the doorway of a cramped, bare room and turned to Ash.

"You wait in there." He gestured to a pair of blue plastic chairs squared beside a scarred wood table.

Ash's eyes grew dark, his mouth dropped, but before he could speak the officer steered him into the room and shut the door. When his gaze connected with Lexi's through the small meshed window in the center of the door, new fear gripped Lexi. The officer turned to her. Cold sweat dampened her neck.

"I think I need to call my mom."

The man ignored her, guiding her down the hall, his heavy-soled shoes thudding against the solid floor until he stopped by an office at the end. The room wasn't like the tiny, sparse one like Ash had been placed in.

"Wait in there," he said, his uniformed shoulders stiff as he gestured to a chair.

Lexi slipped in, settled into a padded gray chair across from a cluttered desk, then waited until he'd shut the door to take out her phone. Two rings later, Dale was on the other end even though she'd called her mom's phone.

"Can I talk to my mom please?" she asked, keeping her voice low.

"What about?" After a few seconds he added, "Why don't you talk to me instead?"

She cringed.

"Please, Dale." She spun her fingers through her hair, willing herself to stay calm, praying her voice sounded normal enough that he'd stop questioning her. "I need to talk to her. No big deal."

"She's asleep. I'm not going to wake— Are you in trouble again?"

Lexi held in a moan. "No. I just need to talk to my mom."

"You sound like— Have you been drinking, Lexi? Are you drunk? Did you take some pills?"

Why had she even bothered calling?

"Forget it." She clicked her phone off so he couldn't call back.

What an epic jerk.

The room was hot, the air stifling. The waiting miserable.

Why *was* she waiting?

What, exactly, was she waiting for?

Tight knots formed at the nape of her neck, gripping her shoulders and creeping down her spine.

Trying to distract herself from the dark tension squeezing its way around her ribs, she looked around. The stuff on the walls looked like props for *Law & Order* — a thick stack of black-and-white wanted posters, some bus schedules, maps. She tucked her legs under her and stared at the brass nameplate on the desk. Detective Waxman.

Her gaze grew fuzzy, pictures of the night tumbling through her head. Events flipped through her mind as though the clips had been spliced together by some guy with ADD. Everything was out of order and blended together.

Did Zeke kill Peter? It made no sense. Did they even know each other? He must've just found him there, already dead. But how could that have happened? Peter hadn't been at the party. Had he?

"Lexi Welks," a voice cut in, saying the words like a label instead of her name.

Lexi blinked and nodded to the tiny woman with short brown hair coming into the room. The woman stopped, stood next to her, patting her right sleeve, then her left.

"Dry," she said softly to herself before bending down to smell the fabric.

By the time Lexi realized what was going on, the woman had moved over to sit behind the desk. She introduced herself as she swept aside a pile of papers, files and clipboards, then leaned in. "You were wearing that shirt when you went into the hot tub?" The woman's coffee-colored eyes glowed so intensely that her cheerful floral blouse looked like a mistake.

"I didn't go into the hot tub." Lexi explained how she'd changed into a suit then covered up with her own clothes, finishing with, "So I was wearing the shirt when I went into the garden room."

The detective nodded and made a note. "Why did you leave the party before the officers arrived?"

"Ash thought it would be a good idea."

"Ash Carpenter is the person you came to the station with. Correct?"

Lexi slid her leg out from under herself and squared her shoulders. "That's right. He drove us here."

Again the woman nodded and made some notes. Then she began a series of questions. After double-checking Lexi's address, age, school and grade, she said, "Tell me what happened." Leaning back, she set a keyboard across her lap. The detective stared at Lexi, her expression still unchanging.

Starting with what had happened after she'd talked to Monica made the most sense. With that resolved, Lexi unwound, describing Spaz and Shortie being themselves in the kitchen. After telling about them, she started to explain the scene at the hot tub, but the desk phone rang, cutting her off.

The detective snatched it up. "Detective Waxman here," she said brusquely, her vigilant gaze skimming across Lexi. She tipped her head while the person on the other end spoke, then murmured, "Yes, she's here." And after a pause, she spoke louder. "You're sure?"

The woman's lips flattened, her eyes poker-faced as she locked gazes with Lexi.

Lexi's stomach clenched as the woman continued to listen silently.

Monica had talked.

Told them about her being with Peter on Friday. If she'd told them that, there was no telling what else she'd said, how far back she'd gone. That girl would do anything to get what she wanted.

Without another word, the detective hung up.

"That's where you were, in the kitchen, when it happened?"

Lexi's heart thudded, that tension around her ribs came back. "I guess so."

The detective made yet another note then asked her to continue telling her what she remembered. By the time she got to the end, she'd remembered most of what had happened, and it seemed so much more real. Zeke was in Cheery Grove. Monica had a secret. And Peter was dead.

"Your account appears to check out. That was one of the investigating officers. Tony Jackson and Scott MacArthur remember you coming into the kitchen, everyone remembers you sitting in the living room, and your clothes are completely dry." Detective Waxman lifted the keyboard off her lap and set it on the table. "We're done for now, Miss Welks."

That was it? No questions about Friday night?

Lexi scooted forward. "I can leave?"

Detective Waxman stood. "I assume since you're in school and a minor, you won't be leaving town."

"No, no, I'm not going anywhere," she replied, getting to her feet.

The woman tipped her head toward the door. "You may leave. We'll be in touch."

Lexi bolted down the hallway, her eyes fixed on the red exit sign shining like a beacon above the automatic doors.

"Hey, hold on," Ash called, jogging to catch up with her.

How could she have forgotten about Ash? Lexi waited until he caught up, then they went through the doors together. The night air was fresh against her skin and breezed away that awful grip on her ribs.

Once they'd stepped into the parking lot, Ash took her arm and stopped her. "It was pretty crappy, huh?"

"No, it was okay. It was a lady. She asked a bunch of questions, made me tell her what happened. She was all business, but she was cool about it."

"The good cop routine," Ash grumbled under his breath, glancing at the doors they'd just come through. "They act like that to make you say stuff so they can use it against you later." He started walking again, scowling as he guided her forward. "She tried it with me, but I didn't tell her a thing."

"She talked to you?" Lexi asked as they reached his Mustang.

The car beeped when he hit the key and the interior lights flashed.

He jerked open the driver's side door. "Yeah, why do you think it took so long for her to get to you?"

She climbed in too, put her bag on the floor and clicked the seatbelt. His face stayed stony, eyes dark.

"Right," she replied, even though she wasn't sure at all about what was going on. Peter dead. It shouldn't be true, but it was. And Zeke? What had happened to him? Monica?

Ash turned over the Mustang's engine. Its rowdy rumble vibrated through the air as he peeled out of the parking lot. The tires squealed as he threw the wheel, taking the turn as sharply as the car would allow. Lexi watched him from the corner of her eye, but his expression didn't give any clue to explain his mood.

Was he pissed because he'd been questioned too?

Sad for Peter?

Scared for Zeke?

She tried to shake off the tension crackling between them, but it was impossible. If she had no idea where it'd come from, how could she make it go away?

Silent minutes crawled by. Hoping to snag his attention as he pulled up in front of her house, she set her hand on his leg and curved her fingers around his thigh. "Thanks again—for everything. I know taking me down there wasn't, um, fun, but thanks."

He looked at her hand, the anger in his expression fading as he set his hand on top of hers. "Let's drive around for a while, okay? I'm not ready to go home." He looked past her shoulder toward her house. "I don't think you are either."

Except for the kitchen, all the windows were dark. What if her mom had woken up and was worried about her? Dale would be right there, saying a bunch of lies, that's what. And she'd have to deal with it. Besides, with the windows all dark, the chance that her mom was awake was slim. "Driving around sounds great."

Ash put his hands on the wheel and hit the gas, the engine roaring once again as he shifted through the gears. They cruised down the empty street to the corner, then turned left. Lexi dropped back, shut her eyes.

"Where do you want to go?"

"Doesn't matter, just driving around is okay." She liked being tucked in Ash's car, away from the world.

"Sounds good to me."

The Mustang hugged the road as he turned, humming as he accelerated.

"You can count on me, you know," he said after a few beats of silence. "I'm good at listening."

Her mouth softened, but still she didn't open her eyes. "I know."

"Then tell me what's going on."

So that's why he'd been mad? He thought the police were playing games with them. "I can't believe Peter's dead. He—"

"No, not that. I saw the way you were looking at your house, Lexi. You need to trust me, tell me what's really happening. With you. With your family."

She peeked at Ash.

It didn't surprise her that he was sensitive enough to realize something was up. Everyone at school knew what he'd been through when his dad died last spring. And that was back before he'd had friends to talk to. Lexi swallowed against the pang of guilt when she thought about how she'd treated him in middle school. It had been too easy to go along with everyone, making fun of him for being so totally awkward and clueless. Sure, most of the teasing had been about random things, like him not getting called onto a team for gym class, or being the only one who cared about an upcoming science test. Still, it had been pretty relentless now that she thought about it. But it must not have hurt him too badly. After his dad died, kids had said he locked himself in his room, but when he showed up at school he was fine. Better than fine, actually. Strong. Mature. With a mysterious air of confidence that set him apart from everyone else.

Thankful to have someone strong on her side who understood what it was like to deal with tough family stuff, she told him the latest about Dale and how sad she was that her mom just let it happen. Over and over. And how it pulled the two of them apart. She finished with the weird stuff Dale had said earlier, about coming back because of her.

Ash sent her a quick glance. "Has he — has he touched you before?"

"No." She grimaced at the thought. "Nothing like that."

"Tell me if he tries anything. Okay?" He smiled, looking as though he wanted to encourage her. That cute dimple creased his cheek and she didn't even have to think about smiling back. He focused on making a left, then added. "I'll help."

"He's not going to do anything like that," she assured him, watching the shops along Grove slide past, dark as tombs. "Besides, now my guard is really up. If he does, I'll be ready this time. I—"

"There are some things even you can't control, Lexi." Ash looked over, all signs of that dimple gone. "Just promise you'll tell me. Okay?"

Nobody had even been so protective of her before. Not even her own mother.

Maybe that was because she'd never let them. Now might be the time to change that. "I will."

He downshifted, made a tight U-turn in the center of the street then started another pass down Grove. They sat silent as they cruised by the empty school lot. Too soon he was headed toward her house.

"Um, well, thanks again for everything," she said, a heavy weight settling over her shoulders as she started accepting that the night had to end. She couldn't go on pretending that scene in the hot tub hadn't happened. News of it was probably already all over town. There'd be a new set of rumors, another wave of drama. Tomorrow she'd have to start answering questions. And facing the truth.

"Anything for you, Lexi. People like us have to stick together." He leaned over, kissed her gently on the mouth. The brush of his lips was too quick, too light. She wanted more.

Needed more.

But he drew back and said good night. "Talk to you tomorrow."

That heaviness wasn't quite as bad now. "Okay."

With him on her side, she could face anything. Jon. Peter. Even her mom and Dale. She grabbed her bag and reached for the door handle.

"Oh, hey," he said, touching her arm. "Why was Monica looking for you?"

Lexi's face flashed hot and a lie tumbled out. "I-I don't know. I, um, never talked to her." She unlatched the door, pushed against it. The night air spilled in and a draft sliced through the cozy interior of the car.

"You didn't, huh?" He dropped his arm, set his hand back on the steering wheel. "That's good. Stay away from her."

Lexi nodded, mumbled goodbye, then climbed out. The door closed with a solid thud, breaking their contact completely. She waved to him from the front porch as he backed out. Within seconds, he was disappearing down the street, swallowed by the night.

After he'd completely vanished, she turned her phone back on.

Just in case he wanted to say goodnight again.

Chapter Nine

Bedtime Stories

Lexi inched the door open, stepped through, then turned to gently push it closed. Once she was inside, she heard the hum of her phone. It came then went, then came again. And again. No way was she going to answer it. She wasn't even going to look. If it was Jazz, she'd understand why Lexi wasn't in the mood to talk. With Ash gone, the loneliness and anxiety had already crept back. All she wanted was to climb into the shelter of her covers and wait for the oblivion of sleep. Tomorrow she'd deal with the fallout from the party. With Monica. Sort out whatever was left of herself.

The house was dark, except for a single red light glowing from the kitchen counter. When she went over to snap off the coffee maker she spotted her mother slumped over the kitchen table, asleep beside an empty Wayne State mug.

Lexi paused, questions crawling through her mind.

Why didn't her mom see she could get someone better than Dale?

How long until she herself snapped, ended up helpless and pathetic too?

Queasiness curled through Lexi's stomach. She couldn't let that happen.

But what if what Ash said was true—that there were some things you couldn't control?

She gently nudged her mom, but she woke with a start anyway.

"Dale?" she mumbled, pushing her hair off her cheeks.

Lexi's heart sank. Of course he was the first person she thought of. "No, Mom. It's me."

"Oh, Lexi. Hi, honey." She looked up with sleep-filled eyes smudged with mascara. Even though she was hurting, she still felt sad for her mom. Over and over she let Dale disappoint her. She rubbed her mom's shoulders, realizing she wasn't going to tell her about Peter until morning. "Go to bed. You'll get a stiff neck sleeping like that."

She pushed herself upright, searching the kitchen with her puffy, tear-stained eyes.

"Go to bed," Lexi repeated, as gently as she could. "It's late."

Defeat lingered in her gaze. "I'm waiting for Dale. I don't know where he is, he hasn't called."

Figures.

"We went to bed, but when I woke up, he was gone." She looked into her empty coffee cup as though she might find some answers in the cold sludge at the bottom. "You go to bed, sweetie. I'm going to wait up for him."

She couldn't remember the last time she'd kissed her mom, but right then she felt so sorry for her that she bent down, placing her lips on her temple. Even though her own world was falling apart, she didn't feel as miserable as her mom looked. And at least she still had the confidence to fight back, to do something.

And now she had Ash.

"You should go to bed, Mom."

"Don't worry about me." She ran her fingers under her eyelashes, trying to wipe away the makeup smudges making her look hollow. "Your mail stack's getting pretty big," she said, forcing her voice to a high, falsely cheerful pitch. "Lots of important-looking college stuff. Why don't you take it up with you?"

Like that matters.

It does matter, she reminded herself.

It's your only way out, away from all this.

"Good night," Lexi called softly, pausing at the bottom of the stairs to grab her overflowing pile of school brochures and test prep postcards.

She bunched the mail together then held it under her elbow as she went to her room. She was alone, but there was no escaping Dale. He'd straightened her things, washed and folded her laundry, carefully made her bed — again. The perfectly tidy room gave the illusion of privacy, the image that everything was right. It made her feel sick.

She passed through the perfect gloom, flipping through the stack of mail. Six college packets and two ads for summer pre-admission programs.

Lexi ran her finger along the edge of the glossy envelope from an out-of-state college. The only way she was going to get that far from Cherry Grove was with a scholarship.

A soft rap on her door made her jump.

"Dale's home." Her mom's bloodshot eyes stared through the dim light. "He says you're having trouble again. Someone was talking about you down at that coffee shop he likes to go to, saying something about an accident with one of the kids from school." Her mom paused. "Are you all right, honey?" She moved into the room, the light from Lexi's desk casting shadows across her face. The frown pulling on her mouth made her look old and tired.

Lexi raised a shaky arm, awkwardly pushing her bangs back. Even if she did want to tell her mom what had happened, she wouldn't know where to start. It hadn't made any difference last time, so why bother? And there was Dale, lingering around somewhere, a threat even though she couldn't see him. "I'm fine, Mom. I stayed up too late, that's all."

"There's too much going on in this town. You need to be more careful." Her mom sighed, then stood a little taller. "Dale's right, you need a curfew."

Fresh anger flowed across the horribleness of the night, but Lexi held still, waiting for it to pool in a place where she could seal it away. Now was not the time to lose it. So she stayed silent, hoping her mom would slump away the way she usually did when Dale was nearby.

Her mom moved back and flipped on the overhead light. "Well, what happened?"

Lexi squinted against the bright invasion. "I'll tell you in the morning. Okay?"

"No." For the first time in ages, her mom pressed for an answer. "Dale wants—I want—to know. Now."

"Really, Mom. I'll tell you everything tomorrow." Lexi kept her voice low, hoping Dale would stay wherever he was instead of coming in and acting like his opinion mattered. "Rehashing it now won't change anything, it already happened."

Slight friction crackled in the room. Lexi found herself half hoping her mom would actually fight back and insist that she tell her everything, show some emotion, some determination, instead of just giving up.

"Mom, *Dale* is what we need to talk about."

"No." Her mom folded her arms across her chest, her elbows poking out of the threadbare robe. "We should talk about you, and what's been going on lately. Why are you involved in all this trouble? What's going on with your friends?"

"If you're not going to talk about Dale, I'm not going to talk at all."

"Why do you want to talk about him? He doesn't have anything to do with any of this."

The strength lingered on her mom's face for a heartbeat then fell and was replaced with confusion and grief. Defeated, she stepped back and touched the light switch. Darkness crowded the room, the door clicked shut, closing off the opportunity for a real emotional exchange once again.

Lexi slipped out of her skirt, let it puddle at her feet, took off her top and tossed it onto her desk. Not the usual jumble she preferred, but it was a start. She still had the swimsuit on, so she peeled it off, threw it toward the laundry basket.

Her mom wasn't going to be much help right now. At least she had Ash.

He was solid and real. Someone she could depend on.

Wearing a plain white T-shirt, she crawled into bed. After staring at the ceiling for what felt like hours, she finally slept.

But it wasn't good sleep.

Questions about Zeke and Monica spun through her mind. Pictures of Peter's limp body and the rush of her own confusion filled her dreams.

Chapter Ten

Green with Envy

Monday after lunch, as Lexi carved a path through the crowded hallway, splashes of red flickered past. And black. Twelve-thirty and she'd just gotten that it was yet another school spirit day. Like wearing Cherry Grove's colors was going to make Peter smile down from heaven. How stupid. And morbid.

She caught her reflection in the floor-to-ceiling window. An uninspired gray V-neck and Old Navy jeans.

No red. No black.

Like she cared.

The usual swarming mixture of people milled around the main offices. Kids wanting passes because they were late coming back from lunch, teachers complaining about the photocopier being broken, delivery guys trying to wheel the giant cart of juice and Gatorade bottles through the crowd. There were even some parents, probably wanting to check on their kids, make sure nothing had happened to them.

Lexi slid in behind three Goths creeping along the walls and tried to blend into the lunchtime chaos. The last thing she wanted was for somebody to spot her on her way in to see Mrs. Howell, one of the counselors.

Kids in class were already avoiding her. Except for Zoë, the boosters were hardly talking to her at all. And worse than that, Jazz had broken down and told her parents about sneaking out of the house. So they'd taken her phone away and sent her, and several weeks' worth of schoolwork, to stay with her grandparents in Montreal.

Lexi reached the inside of the office. The counselor's door stood open, so Lexi dashed in without knocking. Mrs. Howell's head jerked up, a smile crossing her face when their gazes connected.

"Hi, Lexi. I'm glad you came." The counselor took off her glasses, closed the file she'd been reading and laid it on top of an overflowing pile. "When I send for students, I'm not always sure they'll come."

Lexi dropped into the infamous Head-Shrinking Seat, the chair right across from Mrs. Howell. "I didn't know I had a choice." Instead of making eye contact, she looked around, checking out the collection of photographs circling the room. Obviously Mrs. Howell had been all over the world. One photograph was of a group standing in the middle of what looked like a market in some exotic country. The people in the group all looked like total tourists, cameras hanging from their necks and giant hats plopped on their heads. Beside that one was a shot taken on a boat, loads of sunshine brightening the water in the background.

There were several more, and even a picture of Mrs. Howell on a camel in front of a pyramid.

"Must to be nice to run away from home on a regular basis."

The woman smiled but the change in her face was faint, a smile to show understanding, not happiness. "Before becoming a school counselor I taught social studies. I've always suffered from a bad case of wanderlust." She leaned back in her chair. "Maybe I should've been a hobo instead of a school counselor."

Lexi sucked in a deep breath, stared down at her boring Nikes. Her heart thumped and her hands felt weirdly sweaty. Maybe those other kids, the ones who didn't show up when she sent for them, had the right idea. She leaned forward. "I don't really have anything to talk about so maybe I should just get going."

Another of those faint smiles was followed by, "Please stay. I'm glad you came." Then she slipped over and gently shut the door. "A lot has happened in your life lately."

A dead guy and a stepfather back from God knows where probably qualified as 'a lot'. And those were only the things everyone knew about. That night with Monica, parked by the old Westerville field, throwing Jon's bike into the dumpster. Lexi winced. She wasn't going to think about the video camera and all that. "I don't see what there is to talk about, you probably know everything, it's all in the news." And the rest, like that she'd been with Peter on Friday, was now buzzing through the halls. Thanks to Monica, no doubt. The cops were going to find out eventually, so now she was just waiting for them to come to her.

The woman steepled her fingers and tipped her head, looking at her with warm brown eyes. Her gaze wasn't pitying, just thoughtful. "Why don't you tell me how you feel about what happened? I don't know that."

"How should I feel?" Panic had melted away most of her precious control. Her confidence was falling away too. "Sad? Ashamed? Guilty? I'm so confused I can't feel anything."

"Is there any one emotion that stands out?"

Lexi stayed silent and tried to swallow away the lump in her throat.

Mrs. Howell lowered her chin, and her clear crystal chandelier earrings jangled. "Do you blame yourself for what happened?"

Blame.

Now there was a loaded word.

Lexi looked at the beige-carpeted floor. She had to keep herself together. No matter what. "I haven't tried to figure out how I feel." That was the truth. "I feel numb, you know? I hardly knew him. Now he's dead. If Zeke killed Peter, that means I just missed walking in on one guy killing another." She crossed her leg over her knee and stared picking at the worn sole of her sneaker. "Everyone's started calling me the black widow. The guys I had on my auction list made me take them off—like it's some kind of joke. I don't think it's funny."

Mrs. Howell opened her mouth but snapped it shut when a rumble of commotion came from the hall outside. Once it quieted, she said, "No. It's not funny."

Lexi squeezed her legs closer. "And no one knows how Peter died. It's under investigation. Zeke says he didn't have anything to do with it. We shouldn't assume he's lying. Innocent until proven guilty, right?" From out of nowhere, tears welled in her eyes and her fingers started to tingle.

She tried to shut down her wild thoughts, but the cracks in her strength were too wide, and the spiral of emotions seeped through. "I do feel like it's my fault."

"Just because you found Peter doesn't make it your fault."

That was easy for her to say. She didn't have to deal with the stares and whispers. And knowing that she hadn't spoken up when she should have. But that didn't really matter now that he was dead. Right?

"How're your parents handling it? Are they helping you through?"

Lexi's face flashed with heat. She wiped her eyes with the back of her hand, pulled her legs to her chest and wrapped her arms around her calves. Everything that'd happened in the past ten days had left her weak, drained. She didn't have the energy to fight.

So there they were. The memories that always came back when she was weak.

Her dad's funeral.

The annoying way people kept saying over and over how sorry they were. Like that was going to help.

Her mom, spending whole days crying on the couch. Lexi, doing everything she could to get her mom up and moving. Just talking her into doing simple things, like making dinner, had been difficult. But at least she'd felt needed.

Then Dale.

Showing up right about the time she and her mom were getting back on their feet and learning to be a family with just the two of them. And so she wasn't needed anymore. That closeness that'd brought her and her mom together during those months after her father's death, that was gone for good.

The counselor prompted her again. "You mom and dad?"

Lexi set her chin on her knee. "After my mom got married…"

Mrs. Howell leaned forward, setting her hands in her lap. "Your stepfather?"

Lexi's eyes focused on the present. Instead of her memories, she saw the school counselor, gazing softly at her.

Sympathy was something people rarely felt for Lexi. She wouldn't let them. So she opened her mouth to say there was nothing to tell about her stepdad, but truth tumbled out instead. "He gets between me and my mom. He turned her against me."

As soon as the words were out, Lexi braced herself for Mrs. Howell's disbelief, but instead the woman leaned back again and said, "Tell me more."

Part of Lexi wanted to clam up. But another part, the part that had been worn down and wrung out, thought *what the hell*.

The second part won.

She lifted her chin. "He has this way of making everything my fault, making me look like a complete loser. And my mom believes him, listens to everything he says." Lexi dropped her feet to the floor and squared her shoulders. "My mom may be stupid enough to still want him around, but I'm not. I wish he'd leave for good. I hate him hanging around trying to pretend he cares about us."

Mrs. Howell slipped out of her chair and came around to stand near Lexi. "Does your mom know how you feel?"

She'd tried to tell her. Before that, she'd hinted that she hated Dale, but she'd never explained why. She shook her head, understanding for the first time that what she feared most was if she came right out and told her mom what she thought that her mom would take his side. Pick him over her.

The lunch bell shattered the comfortable balance between them, startling Lexi and bringing her back to reality.

She'd opened up, and it scared her. "I better go."

"Wait—Lexi." The woman lightly touched Lexi's arm. "Let me help."

"There's nothing you can do. Peter's not going to come back to life." Lexi got up and backed away. Not from the woman's offer of help, but from the pain threatening to break loose and tear apart what little control she had left. "I don't need any help."

Mrs. Howell took a step forward. "Sometimes just talking helps. I'd love to listen. We can meet again if you like. I'm sure your mom would want to talk too. You should try it, let her know how you feel."

For a split second, Lexi believed her. Maybe her mom would listen, start to understand that Dale wasn't the man she claimed him to be. But years of practice made her snuff out that ray of hope. Believing someone cared, waiting for help. That was a joke with no punchline.

Lexi told the counselor if she wanted to come back, she'd make an appointment. Then she mumbled thanks and left, slipping out the door quickly and without looking back. Sure, for a few seconds it had felt good to put her feelings into words, tell somehow else a tiny bit of what she was thinking. But that didn't mean she had to open herself up for more pain.

Out in the main office, she locked gazes with a familiar pair of eyes. Monica. One of the do-gooder volunteers sorting out yearbook orders.

The other girl looked odd.

Where was the contempt? The constant reminder of their 'friendship'?

Then she realized, it was the way Monica had looked at her when they'd been out together, cruising the streets of Cherry Grove—and beyond. It had been a wild, fearless couple of months. Lexi stalled, mesmerized the other girl's face, caught up in the good parts of those days. Then a guy coming out of one of the other counselor offices bumped into her as he headed for the door. The jolt snapped Lexi out of her confusion and she tore herself away from the once familiar connection she'd shared with Monica. She rushed out of the office, pushing the whole scene out of her head.

No more letting Monica get the best of her, and no way was she going to talk with Mrs. Howell again.

Jazz. She needed Jazz. But that wasn't going to happen. Her parents had made it clear they were cut off.

Ash.

Think about him.

Steady. Kind. Understanding. Sincere and honest. He was more than she'd ever imagined. If she thought about him, she might make it through the day without falling apart.

Chapter Eleven

Big Girls Don't Cry, But They Do Get Pissed

Later that afternoon, sickening déjà vu rolled over Lexi as she came through Taylor's bedroom doorway. Same as the last meeting, Taylor sat in her window seat dressed in a tracksuit — lime green with pink piping this time — and the rest of the boosters were scattered around, wearing their usual casual but planned to an inch of their life outfits. Lacoste, Anthropologie, J. Crew, it was all there.

A difference this time — the expressions on their pretty faces. A mixture of eager speculation and morbid curiosity. A few, like Zoë, actually looked sad. Lexi looked from one booster to the next, wondering what, exactly, was the best way to handle this.

"Hi," Taylor said, ignoring the stupid way Lexi was standing there, awkwardly staring at all of them. "Come on in and sit down. We're waiting for Monica."

At the mention of Monica's name Lexi's stomach lurched, but she forced a smile as she perched on the corner of the bed next to Zoë. "Are you okay?"

Zoë leaned over, speaking softly. "Yeah. Thanks for asking. I'm, it's, well, yeah. I guess I'm all right."

One of the other girls scooted close. "How about you? How're you doing, Lexi?"

"Okay, I guess." It was a lie, but what else could she say?

"Yeah?"

Lexi pressed her lips together and nodded.

Taylor tipped her head and smoothed back her glossy hair. "We're all really concerned about you, Lexi."

She angled back and looked at everyone again. "Well. Thanks." They all stared back at her, their faces expectant. "I'm fine."

Once they caught on to the fact that she wasn't about to dish out a second-by-second account of what it was like to find a dead body, the girls started talking about their plans for the upcoming week. Andrea and Betty Ann went on about going to the mall to look at prom dresses — even though the dance was still months away. Sheryl Banter bragged to anyone who'd listen about Isaac, her latest 'boyfriend'.

Lexi's own plans consisted of avoiding her mom, Dale and everyone else. Except Ash.

Sudden silence snapped Lexi's attention away from her dismal thoughts and she turned to see why everyone was staring. Monica, leaning against the doorjamb, smirking like she'd just been made *America's Next Top Model*, was the cause. As quickly as they'd stopped, everyone started talking again. Not to each other, but to Monica.

"Hi, Monica!" Sheryl said, tossing her feathered brown hair.

Betty Ann got up and did a mock bow. "Awesome outfit, fashion goddess!"

Someone behind Lexi asked, "Where'd you get your hair blown out?"

Monica answered all the questions, smiling as she pulled a chair over to sit beside Taylor.

Right beside Taylor.

Oh.

Yes. Of course.

Monica had been chosen as next year's president and no one had bothered to tell her.

"Okay, let's get going," Taylor said, turning to Monica, her new best friend.

"I don't think we need to discuss the auction," Monica said. "With everything that's happened, it's obviously off."

Everyone nodded, murmuring agreement. Everyone except Lexi, anyway. She sat silently as conversation about the investigation, who the police had questioned, who they hadn't, tumbled around the room. What was happening to Zeke? Nobody knew. Then the topic turned to Peter's funeral and how it was going to be completely — totally — private. Strictly family only. And all the parents were saying no wakes for the kids.

Taylor waved the conversation away with both hands. "Let's focus on what we can do to move ahead. We'll need to make up the money over the summer, which is one of the reasons I've called this meeting. The other, of course, is to make it official — I've recommended Monica to replace me next year. As always, she'll start doing the small duties at first and be completely ready to take over when I graduate."

Bubbles of applause popped all around the room. Lexi patted her hands together, pretending to be happy as her last dream was squashed.

"Okay! Okay!" Taylor and Monica laughed together, their matched smiles toothpaste ad perfect. "I know. It's awesome news! But we don't have time to celebrate right now. Not with everything going on." She lifted her arms to silence the last bit of chatter. As a solution to canceling the auction, Monica suggested we make up the lost money by having a giant garage sale after Thanksgiving or maybe in the spring."

The girls' heads jerked up and down. Monica could've suggested cleaning people's basements and they would've agreed. The other girls exchanged ideas for the garage sale, but Lexi couldn't summon the energy to care. The whole boosters thing suddenly seemed so stupid and pointless. What did it matter now? She let the rest of the meeting buzz around her, waiting as the girls sorted out the details for the garage sale.

The air in Taylor's room was smothering, and she didn't want to be caught alone with Monica. The second the meeting was called to an end, she said goodbye to Zoë and the others nearby then was the first one out. It was rude to leave without saying goodbye to Taylor and the other seniors, but she didn't care what the other girls thought anymore.

She was out of the front door and across the lawn in second. After hopping into Saturn, she checked her rearview mirror. Everyone was bunched up with Monica in the center, laughing and accepting hugs. Lexi pulled away from the curb and hit the gas.

So what that she'd left in a rush?

It wasn't like things could get any worse.

The curves of Taylor's TV-ready neighborhood had more twists and turns than usual. The wide homes flashed past, turning into a beige blur. When her tires squealed in protest at the awkward throw of the wheel, Lexi realized the houses weren't flying by. She was driving at twice the legal limit and gripping the wheel so tightly her knuckles were white.

Screw Monica.

Ditto Taylor.

And the boosters.

Lexi took her foot off the gas, coasting to the next stop sign. She paused, took two deep breaths, then headed toward town. She'd go to the library for a while, get some extra studying in, so she could at least continue to beat Monica where it mattered.

Cruising by the high school, the bright blink of Ash's Mustang caught her eye. The back gym door was propped open. She turned in. Walking across the mostly empty lot, she reconsidered. Too bad she wasn't wearing something better than an old pair of skinny jeans and a ratty ice-blue Champion sweatshirt. No worries. She'd distract him with a flirty smile.

Ash was the only guy in the weight room. His white tee clung to his back, and sweat glistened on his neck. Lexi paused, checking out the band of his white briefs, which almost blended in with his light-gray Nike shorts. Even his pale legs looked strong and muscular. Her gaze crept back up. Yum.

When their gazes connected in the long mirror stretching the length of the weight room, he grinned. He'd noticed her staring at his ass, but she could tell he was more than okay with it.

"Hey, what's up?" he shouted over the blaring Lamb of God.

All pretense of being flirty and fun vanished as Lexi walked toward him. He was her friend. She could be real with him. "Taylor made Monica president."

He switched down the volume, but she could tell he hadn't heard her, so she told him again, adding, "But I'm okay with it."

"You earned that spot. She didn't." He crossed over to pick up some really heavy-looking black plates. "So, no, you're not okay with it."

"Really. I am."

She followed behind him, watching as he positioned the hole of one of the plates at the end of a long bar then slid it on. He did the same on the other side.

"That's nice of you to worry about me," she said, "but—"

"I can't believe Taylor made her president." The second plate slammed into position with a loud crack. "Nobody likes Monica. She's a total bitch and everybody knows it. Even the teachers know it. They just act nice to her because she does what they say."

Lexi took a step back, not quite sure what he was so mad about. Unless he really did care that much about her. "It's not that big a deal," she said, trying to lighten the mood. "Look on the bright side, we'll—"

"There is no bright side. You wanted to be president, you should be president." He angled himself under the bar so it rested across his beefy shoulders, then stepped forward and squatted. Each time he stood, he grimaced and let out a heavy puff of air.

He moved forward then paused, looking over at her. "It matters to you. If there's any way you can make it happen, you should do it. "

Lexi shrugged, still not sure what he was getting at.

"Do it. Whatever you've got, use it."

Lexi waited until he'd dropped the bar back into place to offer, "We'll have more time to hang out this way."

He let out one last hard breath, shoved his hair off his forehead then turned, his gaze softer. "You think?"

"Sure. And—the other good thing. They canceled the auction." Her mouth curved up, her gaze traveling the length of his long, lean body. "Now you don't have to worry about me bugging you anymore."

That made him laugh. Still grinning, he climbed back under the bar, put it across his shoulders again.

Lexi was starting to feel stupid staring at him while he was all sweaty and groaning. "I'll get out of here so you can—"

"Hey, wait. Zeke's around." He paused. "Hang on, you can say hi."

Lexi knew he wasn't in jail or whatever, but the idea that he was out walking around was a shock. Besides, the cops had told her not to talk to anyone, and she was pretty sure that especially meant don't talk to Zeke. Even though she was still wondering what he was going to tell her about Monica. "Nah. You guys have to work out, right?"

"Yeah, I guess you're right." He lowered himself down then grunted as he pushed himself up. "He can't start school until the school board says so, even though the judge is telling them he should be in school."

"That sucks," Lexi said, that image of Peter in the hot tub coming back.

"Yeah. It does. Especially since he moved to get away from the last thing."

Lexi let her curiosity push away that image of dead Peter. "What was it?"

"Just something that happened." He went down then up again. "It totally wasn't his fault."

Lexi took a step back, looking around. Ash and Zeke were way closer than she realized. "What kind of stuff?"

"Lame crap that nobody but parents care about." Ash laughed. "Something about some girl and a video. Know what I mean?"

A girl and a video?

Yeah. She knew what he meant.

Exactly.

"Anyway, it was really bad for him there, but it's going to be great for us because he's the best catcher in the state."

Lexi took her phone out of her pocket, flipping it over in her hand and doing her best to look everywhere except at Ash. "Yeah, yeah, that's great."

"What's wrong? You look weird."

Lexi touched her hair, running her fingers through the strands near her cheek. "No. It's just, well, you look really good doing that."

"Distracted you, huh?" he said, stretching his arms overhead, the edge of his T-shirt riding up, showing more of his hard stomach. Lexi took advantage of his misunderstanding. "Yeah, so I guess I really better get going. I've got some studying to do at the library. Tell Zeke I said 'hi'."

"Right. Don't want to mess with your head. I know those good grades matter to you." He dropped his arms, the crooked smile vanishing as quickly as it had appeared. "Think about what I said. That thing with Monica. Okay?"

Lexi nodded, then with another wave and a last glance at the hard curves of his back, she was out of there and heading to her car. Enough was enough.

She climbed in and typed a text to Monica.

We need to talk.

After she hit 'Send', she headed to the library.

* * * *

Later, still waiting for *the princess* to respond, Lexi leaned hard on the fridge door. Blocks of cheese, piles of yucky-looking pimento loaf and cans of beer filled the shelves. A sour scent drifted forward from somewhere inside. With a quick shove, she closed the door. She couldn't even get something to eat without being reminded of Dale.

Even though it was pointless, she took her phone from her pocket and checked the screen again. Still nothing. A violent shout followed by pitiful screaming burst in from outside. Then a pause, then more shouting. She slipped her phone back into her pocket and peered out between the curtains at the driveway. Dale behind the wheel of his welding truck, her mom clinging to the driver's side door. Her stepdad's thin lips were twisted into a snarl, and he yanked his arm away when her mom tried to touch his shoulder. She was trying to say something but he was waving his hands in her face. After he nearly spat at her, she let go, limping backward.

He backed out, tires squealing, leaves flying, then sped down Cedar. A cloud of dust rose up from the gravel driveway, swirling around Lexi's mom, and she waved her hand in front of her face. Then, with her back slumped and arms folded over her chest, her mom watched him disappear around the corner.

If there was one thing Lexi knew well, it was that rejection tore a person apart. She wanted to wrap her arms around her mom, comfort her. But at the same time she wanted to shake her shoulders, shout 'be glad he's gone, look at how he treats you, look at how he treats me'.

No matter what she did, nothing would change. Her mom would always be the doormat her stepfather trampled. Lexi let the curtain drop as her mom opened the door.

"Hi, honey. How's school today?" Instead of waiting for an answer, she pulled the door shut, heading for the kitchen as though nothing had happened. The only evidence of the truth were the tear-stained red blotches on her cheeks.

Lexi stood stock-still as her mother very calmly opened the dishwasher. When she started rinsing off the morning dishes, Lexi squeezed her hands into fists. Just as quickly, she released the tension and did her best to relax her voice. "Mom? You're going to act like that didn't happen?"

When she didn't respond, Lexi snapped. "He treats you like dirt! He walks all over you, and you let him. Do you like that, Mom? Do you like being treated like that by some useless, manipulating loser?"

Her mom started scrubbing the plates from last night's dinner.

"Do you like the way he treats me? Always in my face? Telling me I'm a loser?"

One at a time, her mom put the plates into the dishwasher. Then she started on the cereal bowls.

Lexi watched, her eyes starting to tear as she waited. *Say something.*

Anything.

How could her mom just take Dale's crap? Didn't she see she didn't deserve it? Where was her pride? What about the two of them?

"Mom, I know you don't want to accept it, but he's using you. Next time he comes home, don't let him in. Please. Tell him to get lost and not come back. Okay?"

Her mom put the last of the plates in, added some detergent then closed the door. After she poked the buttons, the machine started to hum and her mom finally looked at her. "Is that really what you want?"

Lexi let out a breath and nodded.

Her mom pulled out one of the padded kitchen chairs and pointed to the matching one across from it. "Sit down, honey."

Lexi sat, taking in the lines of her mom's face. Finally, the conversation she'd been waiting for.

"I know it isn't always perfect, but Dale and I have been together a long time. He took us in, took care of us. Remember how it was after your dad died? We were all alone, struggling to get by." She ran her fingertip under her eye, wiping away the mascara smudges, something she did way too often. "Sure, Dale and I have our problems, but we've put a lot into our relationship."

"Mom," Lexi forced herself to speak gently, "you've put everything into the relationship, even your self-respect. He hasn't put in anything. He just takes."

"Honey, you can't understand." She looked around the room then turned weary eyes back to Lexi. "You're too young. Idealistic." Tipping her head and again looking around the room, she added, "I understand. I used to be that way too."

Lexi grabbed her mother's elbows, forced their gazes to connect. "I know it was hard when it was just the two of us, but I remember how great things were too. We watched movies, went shopping—even though we couldn't buy anything—it was just the two of us. We were so close, shared everything we were thinking and doing. Then Dale came along and ruined it."

"He did not ruin us. He made us a family."

Praying that Mrs. Howell was right, that her mom did want to hear what she had to say, Lexi pulled all her thoughts together, searching for the perfect words. There were many things she could say, ways to make it sound less awful. None of those sounded right. There was only the truth. "We were already a family—you and me. But with him here, always coming between us, asking questions, making up stuff, he pits you against me. And he harasses me when you're not around. If he went away and stayed away, it could be the same as before. We could—"

"You want me to kick him out of his own home? Divorce him? Your stepfather may not be perfect but I'm not—"

The wall phone rang, cutting the words off. Her mom's gaze flew to it, a desperately hopeful light shining in her eyes. Within a heartbeat, she was on her feet but Lexi was faster. Snatching the receiver, she turned her back on her mom to answer it, and in that split second, Lexi rebuilt her protective wall.

Even as she answered it, she already knew who was on the other end.

"Is your mom there?"

Lexi looked at her mom, opened her hand and let the phone smack onto the linoleum. Her mother's submissive voice followed her to the stairs. Then some mumbled words that sounded to Lexi like an apology.

The apology wasn't to her. A single tear escaped, but she quickly wiped it away.

Her own phone vibrated in her pocket.

Monica. Finally. Her text—

Starbucks by school. Now.

Lexi headed back down the steps as she texted back.

Okay.

Her mom was sitting at the kitchen table, the phone cupped to her ear. No sense in telling her where she was going or even saying goodbye. She grabbed her bag and left.

Chapter Twelve

Why Not to Play with Bad Kids

From her spot in the Starbucks parking lot, Lexi could see Monica, already inside, sipping her drink and tapping on her phone. Her long curly hair was wild and hanging over her face, and she was wearing a boring, oversized black sweater. The look was definitely not up to her usual standards.

The coffee shop was crowded, but there weren't any kids from school around. Thank God. Because she did not need to be seen talking to Monica. Lexi climbed out and headed for the door. From her table by the window, Monica spotted her coming. Her chin dipped down in a slow nod.

Inside, Lexi exchanged looks with the girl, crossed to the counter and took a spot behind a woman who looked to be some kind of banker or something. Then again, it was Cherry Grove, so her gray tailored suit could just be what she put on to run some errands. Corny jazz, maybe Dean Martin or Frank Sinatra, drifted down from the overhead speakers, mixing with the chatter of the people in line. If Lexi's world hadn't been in chaos, it would seem kind of cool. But as it was, she felt like a character in a movie, playing the role of a normal girl ordering a chai tea.

"Thanks for coming," Monica said. She'd come up behind Lexi and was standing so close Lexi could smell the spicy vanilla lotion she always wore. The scent triggered a flash of memories. The good ones, the things they'd done in the beginning. Driving around, listening to music. Lying in the overgrown outfield grass of the hidden Westerville baseball diamond, telling each other all their dreams, who they'd had crushes on and what clothes they would buy if they could get whatever they wanted.

Lexi turned, her anger fading a little as she looked in the other girl's eyes. She was stuck in this disaster too. "Heard anything more from him?"

"That's what I want to talk about."

The guy behind the counter set Lexi's tea out, so she picked it up and followed Monica back to the table in the corner.

Lexi waited until they were both seated, then asked, "Did you get another text?"

"No. I didn't and I'm not going to. But I know why." Monica pushed her drink aside and leaned close. "Listen. Listen to everything I have to say before you say anything." She leaned in still closer, urging Lexi to do the same. Once Lexi's elbows were nearly touching hers, she continued. "Something's not right with Ash. And—"

"I don't want to talk about Ash."

"Listen," she said with such force it was almost a hiss. "Think about it. He's messed-up. I—"

"You're one to talk about somebody being messed-up. And I only know part of it." A dry laugh rumbled up Lexi's throat as the fragile connection to the good part of their past evaporated. "Zeke was going to tell me something about you. What was it?"

"Zeke? You've got to be kidding." A flicker of Monica's usual nasty attitude flashed in her eyes, but there was no edge in her words when she replied. "How the hell should I know what he was going to say? And who cares?"

"Obviously you care or you wouldn't be here. So you definitely know. You know because you're right in the middle of everything going on."

Monica leaned back, squinting. "Oh, hell no."

"Why does Zeke hate you?" Lexi asked, lifting her eyebrows.

For several long seconds, Monica didn't move. She didn't even blink. The cheerful jazzy music and the cozy whirr of coffee beans in the grinder sounded more out of place than ever as the girl sat there, her face a mask of nothing. Finally she moved, sliding forward ever so slowly. "We need to talk about Ash."

It was Lexi's turn to lean back. "The auction is canceled. What does Ash have to do with any of this?"

Monica pushed her hair out of her face and looked directly into Lexi's eyes. "He's right in the middle of this. Think about it. Who is connected to all of these people—Peter, Zeke, Jon, even Coach Filpot?"

Lexi considered the list. They were all connected to baseball, but so what? "For one thing, Ash doesn't really know Zeke all that well."

"That's not true. He knows Zeke from a couple baseball camps, and he doesn't like him. Even though he's acting like he does." Monica picked up her cup and drummed the fingers of her other hand across the top. "Actually, he hates Zeke."

"That's bull. He got him invited to Zoë's, and they were working out together."

Monica took a sip of her drink, set the cup back down, then tapped her fingers across the top again. "Did you stop to consider why he brought him to Zoë's?"

"So he could meet the kids from school, because he's new here, because he got in trouble at his old school and because Ash is actually nice and cares about people." But even as she said it, she was already beginning to think Monica was right. What had Ash said when they'd been talking about Zeke in the school weight room? And if the two of them were such great friends, why hadn't Ash been with Zeke? When Zoë 'introduced' Lexi to him, Ash had been nowhere in sight.

Lexi sat back and looked out of the window. It was all the usual stuff out there, minivans, people coming and going, all carrying their steaming paper cups. How could everything look so normal?

"And what about Z makes him likeable? Seriously, we were just goofing around with him. Did you really like him? Think he was a good person?"

"No, I guess not," she replied softly.

Monica laughed, a low noise that sounded more like a snort.

"He's not really anything like Ash."

"I don't know about that."

Monica didn't know Ash like she did. Her opinion on him didn't mean a thing. But Zeke? Yeah, they both knew him. Turning back to the table, Lexi looked at Monica and added with an ironic laugh, "I get what you're saying. Zeke's pretty much a total jerk. Why were we hanging around him anyway?"

"Fun at the time. He sold to us. Did whatever we wanted. Those were all the reasons we needed."

Lexi nodded, took a sip of her chai, remembering the drinking and craziness of the summer. The more she thought about those times, the more her stomach tightened. "We weren't such great people at the time, either."

"Yeah. That's true." Monica's usual haughty hostility was gone. "It's all over now. Over and done with. We're all moving on, headed in different directions."

That was pretty Zen sounding, especially for Monica, who'd always been a here-and-now type person. Was it possible she actually regretted that stuff too? Really did want to leave it behind? "What's Zeke got against you?"

Monica shifted in her chair and looked around the shop. Staring blankly at the line by the counter, she pulled in a deep breath and let it out, then started drumming her fingers across the top of her drink again.

The shop was buzzing with people and music so there was probably no worry about being overheard. "Tell me," Lexi said. "Then I'll listen to what you wanted to say about Ash."

Monica's gaze came back to Lexi. Her eyes were clear now, sharp. "Okay. But not in here."

"Seriously?" Lexi waved her hand at all the people not paying any attention to them.

Monica's only response was to grab her bag and stand.

At least she was finally going to get some answers. Lexi got to her feet. They tossed their cups in the trash can by the door.

Outside the wind had picked up and dry brown leaves were swirling in the breeze. The sun was still bright, reflecting off the cars in the parking lot. Out in the street a yellow VW Beetle slowed then the horn sounded. Monica grabbed her hair, holding it off of her face as she looked over at the driver. The girl's arms shot out of the window, slicing through the air as she yelled, "Hey, Monica!"

Monica waved back, grumbling under her breath, "Don't act like we're together."

Lexi agreed, totally, so she hung back then started walking in the other direction. Once the Beetle turned the corner and squealed off, they started walking toward the school.

Once they were about a half block from Starbuck's, Monica moved closer to Lexi so they could walk side by side. "I'm the one who got Z kicked out of his old school. It wasn't really the school that kicked him out. It was the school board, you know, all the parents that are supposed to run everything. One of the parents, the board president, especially wanted him gone." Monica's face was tight, her gaze straight ahead.

Lexi stayed quiet to see what else she'd say. They walked along with the rumble of traffic humming around them until Monica continued, "That's why the school board here is so against him coming to school. That guy must've told our school board what happened and then the thing with Peter, and, well, his life is a disaster."

"What did you do exactly?"

They reached the end of the block and crossed the street. The school parking lot stretched out in front of them, dotted with a few leaf-covered cars along the edges.

Monica replied with an eerie casualness, "One night he left his Facebook page open when he went out to smoke, and I posted one of the videos on his page."

Lexi tripped on the curb, righting herself just in time to step over another jagged edge in the sidewalk. When she spoke, her voice was a raw whisper. "Which one of the videos?"

"One of the back room ones. You know the ones."

Of course she did. She'd been in that very back room, in front of that very video camera, lifting her shirt and wiggling just so he'd sell to them.

"Turns out, Z, dumbass that he is, has parents on his Friends list. One of them was the girl's dad and he's the president of the school board." Monica shrugged, like it was no big thing. "Guess the dad didn't want the whole world seeing his precious daughter flashing her boobs for some camera."

Lexi stopped walking, the tea in her stomach turning sour and thick. "Everyone in her school must've seen it."

Monica leaned on a small tree beside the sidewalk. Her feet disappeared into bright, fiery leaves. "Nah. It was only up for a couple hours. But what's the big deal? It's just her boobs. And you couldn't see her face. They only knew it was her because of the necklace she had on. A cross from her daddy, how sweet."

All worry about them being seen together or being overheard vanished and Lexi's words came out loud, shrill enough to be carried on the wind across the parking lot. "What's wrong with you? Why did you do that?"

Monica grabbed at one of the few leaves still on the tree's branches, yanked it off, then tossed it into the wind. "I was mad."

"That's not enough reason."

"Whatever." Monica kicked an empty Styrofoam cup on the ground, and it rolled into the street. A car zipped by, smashing it. Another car went by and the crushed cup flew into the air, mixing with some leaves stirred up by the traffic. The flattened cup broke into pieces. Some of the bits floated into the road, one hunk landed back in almost the same spot by Monica's feet.

Once the traffic cleared and it was quiet again, Lexi moved closer to Monica. "What about the girl? You don't even know her."

Monica picked up the flattened hunk and crushed it, twisting it in her hands until tiny white bits scattered the ground.

"You don't have anything to say? That was a seriously shitty thing to do."

She watched the white bits float around for a while then looked up. "I guess I know that now but I can't undo it. The dad wanted it kept quiet, stuff got worked out, and Z is fine. Nobody cares, and he's still in baseball, which is all that matters to him." She waved her hand and took a few steps away from the mess she'd made.

"What about the girl?"

"I'm sure she's fine too. Probably better than fine. Nothing like a good scandal to get people's attention. And she has pretty nice tits, and now all the guys know it. Her phone has probably been blowing up ever since." She laughed. "Maybe she should thank me."

"You're disgusting." Like she had too many times already, Lexi wondered why had she ever gotten involved with Monica. What had pulled her into the girl's disgusting web? "Didn't it occur to you that we could've gotten in huge trouble? Now, because of this mess, it could all come back and we could still get in trouble." She couldn't stand being near the other girl for a second longer so she bolted, marching away toward the school.

Within seconds, Monica was right behind her. "We? I didn't hook up the nasty cam."

Truth. The one hideous truth that was never, ever going to go away.

Somehow it'd been Lexi doing all the work while Monica cheered her on. That was obvious now. How had she missed it at the time?

"Are you going to listen to me now?" Monica asked over her shoulder.

Lexi was still reeling from the reality of her situation, but there was no stopping now. She had to see this conversation through to the very bitter end. "Fine. Go ahead."

"I know you won't tell anyone this, because...well, because." Monica wrinkled her nose and laughed. "I just know you won't." She stopped laughing but her face stayed twisted as she continued. "Something's wrong with Ash. I think he has Jon as his prisoner or something."

Lexi staggered to the side, her head spinning as she tried to make sense of that ridiculous statement. "What are you talking about?"

"Ash." Monica grabbed Lexi's arm. "He's messed-up, and he has Jon."

"What do you mean 'he has Jon'?

"He's kidnapped him, he's holding him somewhere."

She jerked her arm away and started walking again. "That's insane."

Again Monica was right behind her, matching her stride step for step. "No, it isn't. Not if you stop and think through everything that's happened. After you consider it all, you'll see it even makes sense."

The girl was worse off than Lexi realized. "You don't even know Ash."

"Yeah, I do. I know him a lot better than you. We were in science club together."

Lexi threw her a doubtful look. "Science club? Oh, yeah. So the two of you were best friends for five minutes while you washed out some beakers together."

"I've been following him."

The girl was totally unstable.

"Something is seriously wrong with him. He drives around, acting weird. He spends hours and hours in there," she said, pointing to the small square building next to the school they had used for science club. It was a brick structure, something anybody could easily overlook. But just because it looked boring didn't mean something sinister was going on inside. Monica was obviously trying to stir up trouble in the weirdest way possible.

"He goes in there. I'm telling you, it's true. I have pictures." She pulled her phone out. "I'll show you."

"I don't want to see them." Lexi flicked her wrist at the phone in Monica's hands. "You don't know what it's like to lose someone. If he does go in there, he probably does it because he misses his dad."

They were nearing the edge of the school parking lot and Monica was staring at the little building, her gaze skimming across the three small windows. "It's more than that. Ash's dad pushed people, he gave us something to work toward. With him gone, it's like nobody knows what to do next. All that energy and thinking, without direction, it isn't a good thing. Not at all."

Something wasn't adding up. "Explain this to me. Because you were in science club together you decided to follow Ash, and because he went into that building a lot you decided he has Jon."

"No. I decided to follow him because I knew you were going to try to get him to sign, and I wanted to figure out a way to screw that up."

At least that sounded honest.

They were into the school parking lot now, and Lexi scanned the area. She really didn't want to be seen talking to Monica, and she was surprised Monica wasn't worried about being seen with her. After all, if they were going to be spotted, this was the most likely place. Still, she couldn't simply walk away. "Why are you telling me this?"

"You need to know so you can decide what to do."

"I want to go to the cops and tell them what we know about Jon and be done with it." That's what she wanted, but now thanks to Zeke that video camera crap was resurfacing. Could she take the chance of coming forward, drawing attention to herself? Admitting she'd known some things all along but stayed quiet was going to make her look suspicious—and with good reason.

"Don't go, Lexi," Monica said, her eyes suddenly soft and pleading. "Wait. I can prove Ash knows something."

They were walking side by side now. Lexi looked over, shaking her head. "Ash doesn't know anything."

"Wait. One day. That's all I need to prove it to you. If you wait, I'll go with you to the cops. We'll tell them together. Everything, all of it. Or whatever you want to say. Okay?"

Chapter Thirteen

Why Do You Want to Go?

The next night, Lexi sat on her bed, staring into her closet, looking from one hanger to the next.

Too boring.

Too loud.

Too middle school.

Nothing was right for going out with Ash. She checked the clock—twenty-five minutes until he'd be there. She had to pick something—the breezy tailspin skirt or embroidered Hopscotch jeans?

From the gray look of the sky, she couldn't tell if it was going to rain or if the clouds were going to blow off in the heavy wind. Stupid Midwestern weather. Made it impossible to know what to wear.

She also had her mom and Dale to deal with. Downstairs, snuggled on the couch as if they were the most ideal couple ever. Obviously her mom had decided to forget the driveway scene with Dale and that touching heart-to-heart conversation they'd had in the kitchen afterward.

The idea of her mom contentedly wrapped in Dale's wiry arms frustrated the hell out of Lexi. It also hurt way more than she could handle.

Less than an hour ago he'd sat at the dinner table, covering his plate with huge wads of tuna casserole and cucumber salad. He'd gone on about the baseball team's suffering morale, how he'd run into Ash and how Ash had gone on and on about Zeke, the amazing catcher who was going to fix everything now that he was in the clear.

Then he'd started in on Lexi.

Who did she eat lunch with?

What did she do after school?

How were the other boosters doing?

She wanted to hate her mother for just sitting there while she got picked apart. Her entire life would be easier if she managed to get it through her head that her mom was always going to pick Dale over her, but no matter how hard she tried, she just couldn't give up on wanting to be close to her again.

Lexi flipped open her phone and clicked to the shot of Ash she'd taken at Coach's funeral. Even bummed out, he looked in control. Like the whole world could fall apart and he'd still be there. But looks could be deceiving, and you can't ever believe people are who they say they are. She'd learned those things the hard way.

Did that mean Monica could be right?

The idea that Ash had kidnapped Jon was ridiculous, obviously. But if Monica had been following him, what had she seen? There was also the very real possibility the girl was simply saying that stuff to mess with her.

She was probably jealous that Lexi had gotten close to Ash while she had nobody.

She clicked to the shots she'd taken that day they'd gone for coffee. They made a perfect couple, happy and relaxed with plenty of simmer zipping between. They both knew more closeness was going to happen. It was only a matter of when. Lexi had no intention of waiting any longer than necessary. Once they got through all this mess she was definitely going to do something about getting closer to Ash.

She flipped through a couple more pictures from that day they'd gotten coffee. Her favorite was one of Ash smiling straight at her, his eyes clear and honest.

Integrity.

That's what made him different from everyone else.

Each time he'd acted strangely, like that day in the gym when he was being really hostile about Monica, he'd had good reason. And he believed in her, he'd never blow her off the way her own mom had, or be a complete jerk like Dale.

Dale. The never-ending pain in her ass.

Even though the cops had found alcohol in Peter's body, so they didn't have to worry about some serial killer on the loose, it had still taken forever to get Dale to agree to 'let her go out'. The cops had even done a press conference, telling everyone in Cherry Grove that it was time to stop being afraid and "go back to the business of living" but Dale thought he knew better. He'd only finally given in because she was going out with Ash and she'd implied that since she and Ash were going to be a couple, and Ash and Zeke were friends, well, she had some influence. Influence that she could use as she saw fit. Oh yes, then all of a sudden he'd decided the cops knew what they were talking about.

Thank God her mom and Dale hadn't heard the rumor that Monica was missing. Taylor was going nuts, texting everyone, asking if they'd seen Monica but telling them to keep quiet at the same time. Like asking the question too loudly could make the worst-case scenario true. The strategy didn't make sense to Lexi, but she knew nothing bad had happened, so she wasn't worried. The real reason Monica was in hiding—that twenty-four hour agreement. Time was up, and after her night with Ash, she'd decide whether or not she was going to wait for Monica to come out of wherever she'd run off to or go to the cops alone. She smiled. Until that time, she had Ash to take her mind off everything. That and lay the groundwork for what she wanted to make happen with him once everything settled and she was no longer in the spotlight. After curling her hair, she shimmied into her jeans and a no brand, sky blue, mohair sweater. An actually decent thing her mom had brought home from a garage sale. The soft fur collar caressed her chin and the neckline dipped low enough that when she bent over Ash would be able to see the edge of her push-up bra.

By seven-forty Lexi was dressed.

Waiting downstairs was out of the question—they were down there. So she stood at the top of the stairs, her heart thumping as she listened for the roar of Ash's Mustang.

Her mom's laughter floated up the stairs. Dale's know-it-all low rumble followed. Lexi was glad she couldn't hear whatever Dale was explaining. He thought he was so brilliant.

Hurry, Ash.

Time passed. Edgy nerves tightened her skin. She checked her texts then scrolled through Facebook. Took a quick look at Twitter and Instagram.

Hurry up, please.

He was late.

Maybe he wasn't coming.

No, he was late. That's all.

"Come on in, Ash!"

Crap. She'd been too distracted to hear his car. She scrambled down the stairs, taking them two at a time and using the handrail to hop quickly.

Still she didn't get there fast enough. Ash was already handling Dale's Welcome Wagon routine, shaking hands and answering stupid questions about the upcoming season and how his strength training was coming along. When Dale finally let go and stepped back, Ash stood tall and shoved his hands into the back pockets of his jeans.

From the bottom of the stairs, Lexi cast him an apologetic glance.

He nodded, telling her he got what she was saying.

"Hi, Ash," her mom said from the couch. "Do you really think it's a good idea? Going out, I mean."

Ash offered a parent-friendly nod. "We'll be fine, Mrs. Welks."

Lexi stepped over to stand beside him, moving close enough for her shoulder to brush his arm. He smelled great. A mixture of spicy freshness. The scent was deep enough to be good for a guy but not overwhelming like some of the sprays other guys used. Being so near him made her that much more anxious to get out of there. But now her mom was fussing over Ash, asking him pretty much the same questions Dale just had.

After Ash answered them all, she looked over at Dale, a frown replacing the too-friendly smile she'd had just seconds ago. "I don't know," she said. "What do you think?"

"Ash is going to be the team captain this season," Dale said, being his usual asinine self by assuming that if a guy was a jock he could do anything. But for the first time ever, Lexi didn't care about Dale's stupidity, and actually found herself hoping her mom would do her usual thing and accept what he was saying. Dale grabbed Ash's shoulder, shaking him so vigorously that the room started to smell like burnt solder instead of Ash. "He'll look out for our girl. No worries at all."

"I don't know. Something doesn't feel right," her mom added softly, picking at the hem of her lemon-yellow cardigan. "Why take the chance? You two could stay here, watch a movie or something. Dale and I can go upstairs. How's that sound?"

Dale didn't give her the chance to reply. He turned his know-it-all face to Lexi's mom, slicing his wiry arms through the air as though he could dismiss her concerns just like that. "With the curfew back in place, everything's fine." Then, glancing at Ash, he added, "And it looks like she's showing some sense for once, sticking with Ash instead of tramping around with a different guy every week."

Her mother leaned forward, directing her words to her husband. "Dale, it's not like that. Lexi's a good girl and you know it."

That was the first time she could ever remember her mom defending her. She almost smiled, until she spotted the angry red flush creeping up Dale's neck. Her mom shrank back into the cushions.

Ash tapped her arm, tipped his head toward the door. She got the message. As she gently pushed the front door closed, Dale's words cut clean through the wood. "Don't you realize I know that girl better than you do?"

Ash's jaw flexed as he turned his car's ignition and started down Cedar Street.

Who could blame him? It was like he'd walked onto the Jerry Springer set.

How totally embarrassing.

She should apologize or something.

But, as always, he was one step ahead. "Parents are freaks," he said, looking away from the road to give her a quick smile. "Forget it."

After the way she'd blurted out her feelings about Dale to Mrs. Howell, there was no telling what she might say to Ash. Plus, she didn't want her dysfunctional family setup to be the focus of their night. So she just said, "Yeah. Thanks."

They drove along in silence for a few minutes. Just like she had after the disaster of Zoë's party, she relaxed into the seat and watched the world go by. It seemed that most of the people around Cherry Grove weren't ready to follow the police chief's advice about getting back to normal because the streets were empty. Lexi didn't mind. For a while at least, it was going to be just the two of them.

He braked at the corner, right in front of the school, then turned. When he accelerated, shifting through the gears with ease, the humming engine made the car vibrate. The square, white houses across from the football field whipped by, glowing beyond the mostly bare trees lining the street. Most of the houses were dark, except for the occasional porch light casting a thin bright pool across a lawn. It would have been cool looking if it weren't kind of creepy. When Ash hit the gas again, she asked, "Where're we going?"

"Someplace quiet. So we can be alone." He took a left onto Grove, slowing only a little as he cut through the intersection.

The milk carton houses disappeared and the bigger trees surrounding Morgan Lake took their place. The thinning limbs reached for the sky, grabbing the darkness, holding it away from the thick pines in the back that blocked the view of the park from the road. Finally Ash eased off the gas and slowed to turn onto the narrow gravel road that led back to the park surrounding the lake.

The crunching of Ash's wide tires stopped when he parked in the far corner of the empty lot. He looked over, raised his eyebrows and made a spooky ghost sound, then laughed at his own silliness. "Kind of Blair Witch, huh?"

Lexi laughed lightly as she smacked his arm. "Oh, shut up, I'm not afraid of a bunch of trees."

"Good." He stretched back, reaching for a heavy green blanket on the back seat.

The nasty-smelling thing rubbed against Lexi's cheek as he yanked it between the two front seats. Its musty scent filled the air inside the car and its dust made Lexi sneeze. "Sick!" She sniffled as she pushed it away from her onto Ash's lap. "What is that thing?"

He laughed, swinging open his door then shoving the blanket out. "It's an old army blanket. Guess they didn't worry too much about whether or not it felt good. It's super sturdy—really warm. Great for all kinds of things."

Lexi climbed out, then pushed the door closed with a solid thud. Outside the car, he hit the key fob to lock the car then tossed the dark stinky mass over his right shoulder. "Come on, let's go over by the lake."

From the back of her mind, something nagged at her. It was a faint thought, half-formed but persistent, like she was trying to remember something. Uncertainty distracted her, filling her mind with questions. What was it? Who was it about? Monica? Jon? Zeke? Something her mom had said? Maybe it was just a homework assignment she needed to finish. Or some lingering aggravation from Dale's dumb comments. *Never mind*. She wiped her mind clear. She wanted to be with Ash, and he wanted to be with her. That was all that mattered, and whatever it was, she'd remember eventually.

They started to walk toward the lake. The breeze had completely died down. Each footstep was crisp with the sound of leaves crunching underfoot. She fell into step beside Ash, he wrapped his left arm around her waist, and they passed the silent trees. In the distance cars hummed, but other than the distinct thud of their feet, not a single sound came from nearby. Not even the rustle of a twig.

For now it was just two people alone. Together.

She eyed the coarse blanket bunched across Ash's shoulder with new insight. She knew he'd felt the zing of chemistry between them, but she'd been assuming he'd been thinking what she had — they needed to wait until things calmed down before they acted on it.

Then she realized — as far as the citizens of Cherry Grove were concerned, things had calmed down. Back to normal, that was the public message.

Acting on her feelings for Ash might be tricky, with the lingering stress about Jon and that idiocy with Monica and the back room videos, but going with what she wanted would be more natural than fighting it. If she held off, how would she explain it to Ash? And if she rejected him, she might not get another chance.

When they reached the lake, Ash tugged her over to one of the benches.

Lexi pulled away and took a step back. "Isn't this where Coach died?"

"Maybe. I guess I don't know for sure," he replied, spreading the blanket across the seat. "It's still a decent spot. Away from everything, everyone."

He came over and took her hand, and she let him pull her to the bench. When he set his palms on her shoulders and pressed, she went down willingly.

He was right. They couldn't see any of the houses or nearby stores. Better still, nobody could see them. Complete privacy.

Tiny, soft ripples rolled across the water. A fine layer of fog drifted across the calm surface dotted with leaves and a few small sticks. Lexi watched, waiting for the flip of a fish or the bubbles from a turtle hopping off a log. Nothing. Just the gentle solitude. She tucked away her reluctance about sitting on the coach's death bench, nestled close enough to smell Ash's spicy freshness, then let go of the tension in her shoulders. "This is just what I needed. Thanks for bringing me here, Ash."

The trees shadowed his face but she was sure a smile crossed his lips. But if he'd smiled, where was that cute dimple? "Of course," he whispered as he laid his arm across her shoulders. "It's part of the plan."

The plan?

She turned her face back to the lake but watched him from the corners of her eyes. She knew Ash was a thoughtful guy, more mature than the rest, but that seemed weird even for him. Was he trying to be romantic? Letting her know he'd been thinking of her?

It was kind of an odd thing to say, but so what? Lexi snuggled deeper into his arm and told herself to stop overthinking everything and enjoy the moment. What she wanted was to be with Ash and forget about the things she couldn't control. Monica's drama and that scene at her house with Dale threatened to ruin everything. She was letting that angst blur her feelings.

Not anymore.

Concentrate on this. Focus on now.

As her thoughts shifted back to Ash, she noticed a tiny change in him. Something she would've missed if they hadn't been hanging out together. His left arm was still around her, but his right arm was flexing restlessly, his fist clenching, going loose then squeezing shut again. His gaze kept circling the lake, skimming across the thin mist floating on the water.

"What was your stepdad saying about...?"

Not that. "Something stupid, I'm sure." Looking up at him from under her lashes, she added in what she hoped was a flirty voice, "I thought we weren't going to talk about that."

"Maybe we should." His voice was strained, his fisted hand resting on his thigh as he looked down at her. "It was something about you."

She dipped her shoulder in, pressed her body closer, trying to get him to stop thinking about bigmouth Dale and the mean thing that he'd said. Because if he did keep thinking about that nasty comment, Ash was going to realize that in the beginning, she'd been trying to use him. Mostly all she'd wanted was his name signed on a sheet of paper.

Lexi chanced a longer glance. The muscles along Ash's jaw were tight and he was staring straight ahead.

She had to get him to think about something else. She smashed her boobs against him, murmuring, "Maybe—"

But that was as far as she got, because just as she was about to nuzzle his neck, he grabbed her elbows, jerking her up sharply. "Now I remember." His narrowed gaze raked across her face. "Something about you going out with a different guy every night." He shoved her arms higher, making her slide forward, lifting her off the bench. "I want to know exactly what you did. With Peter. Zeke? Who else?"

She gasped. "I didn't do anything with either of those guys." That wasn't exactly true, she'd done some stuff with Zeke, but not in the way Ash meant.

"Who then?"

He sounded like Dale.

"All of them?" His hot breath grazed her cheek, his fingers squeezing her bones. "I should've figured it out. You'd do anything just for a signature."

Finally, she found her nerve to speak up for herself. "Where is this coming from?"

All traces of the guy she'd thought she'd known were gone from his face.

He sneered. "Maybe you are like that bitch Monica."

Lexi fought against his grip and the idea that she was anything like Monica. "No. I'm not." But even as the words fell from her lips, she started to wonder if she'd been lying to herself. She'd done what she'd done. *A user is a user, after all.*

The sneer faded and his voice was less harsh as he asked, "Then why won't you use what you have against her?"

Because it'll take me down too.

Should she tell him he was right, that she'd talked to players to get them to sign? Worse still, she'd done a little more than talk. Been ready to do a little bit more. But if she admitted that, the other truth about her being ready to manipulate him in the same way was just a step away. She scrambled through her thoughts, trying to grasp how the conversation had gotten so ugly so quickly. What was Ash trying to do? Clear the air?

"That's all in the past." His razor-edged whisper cut the air. "You won't be hanging around like that anymore."

He let go of her arms, swung back, grabbed the foul blanket, wrapped it around her and used it to pull her to him. It happened quickly, all in one motion, so now she was pressed against his chest, his arms a hard, tight bind around her.

Unbelievable but true, Monica was right.

Ash was nasty. And a manipulator like Dale.

With all the strength she had, she got her hands up between them, planted her palms on his chest and shoved. His arms spiraled and he wobbled for a few seconds until he grabbed the back of the bench. She scrambled to her feet, her muscles trembling with anger and determination.

Fueled by anger, guided by instinct, she took off. Flying through the fog forming among the pines, her legs sliced through the gray mist. Behind her, Ash shouted her name, his voice sharp with anger.

She raced on.

He yelled again, louder, more desperate.

She kept running.

Harder.

Faster.

Deeper into the pines where it was darker, the ground more uneven.

Her heart thumped heavily, thrashing deep in her ribcage like a wild dog. Puffs of breath steamed from her lungs, and each inhale pinched her throat. She ran on, sucking in air as twigs smacked her face. On she went, spinning through the darkness. Fallen branches reached for her ankles as she tumbled through the night, kicking her way through the leaves and sticks.

From behind, Ash called her name again. His voice had changed, become more calm. Like he thought he could fool her into stopping, coming back to him. Of course she didn't stop. She ran faster. He kept coming. The thumping of his footsteps got louder as he closed in behind her. Still she pounded ahead, carefully placing her feet so she wouldn't fall.

Again he yelled her name, his voice that much closer.

Then he howled. And went silent.

He'd fallen?

Could she get that lucky?

Hope glowed inside her but she couldn't waste time looking back so she raced on, picking up more speed as she reached the parking lot. The pavement was smoother, made it easier to run, so she moved even faster. The hammering of her heart forced her on through the clammy fog, her legs spinning hard as she headed for the road. Sharp puffs of breath came from deep inside her, giving her the power to keep going.

About the time Lexi reached Grove Street, Ash's Mustang growled in the distance. She slowed, listening to the car's engine and looking for places to hide if he came after her. But instead of growing louder, the sound faded.

He was gone.

She slowed to a jog, then a quick walk, waiting for her chest to stop heaving. As her breath returned to normal, the muscles in her legs started to tremble. Her face flashed hot. Her lips quivered. The reality of what had just happened sank in and traitorous tears rolled down her cheeks. She swiped them away.

Stupid. She'd been so stupid.

Stop crying.

He was like all the others.

An opportunistic ass.

She continued on down Grove, past the lively restaurants. Her breathing was still sharp and painful, but more from panic and rage than the running. Her wrists stung from where he'd grabbed her and there was a red patch on her right forearm.

Tears of shock gave way to quaking anger.

She'd opened up to Ash, started to trust him, and he'd treated her like crap. It was the same thing that had happened with Monica, only with Monica she'd been part of it—wanted to be part of it. It was past time to get her life together and move on once and for all.

She stalled at the corner of Pine and braced her hands on her knees, gulping a few last steadying breaths. Finally her breathing was back to normal. When she stood back up, she caught a glimpse of the police station. She'd thought she was lucky, having Ash with her after Peter's drowning. She blinked against the bright light gleaming across the parking lot. That night had been warm and foggy too.

The double doors of the station swung out and a cop strolled through, pulling a pack of cigarettes from his chest pocket. He lit up right about where Ash had parked his Mustang. Looking at the spot made her remember that hostile edge in Ash's voice. It'd seemed strange then, him getting so upset about being questioned too, but she'd been so caught up in the shock of Peter's death she'd easily reasoned it away.

How much longer was she going to be able to hold back the secrets? Who was she protecting, anyway?

She pulled out her phone and texted Monica, informing her that she was going to tell the cops what she knew about Jon's last night and what they'd done with his bike. A response came right away.

Meet me at your house. I'll be right there. We'll go together.

Lexi looked from the screen of her phone to the station. Yeah, she could go now. Walk right in and get it over with. But it would be easier to go with Monica, explain everything together and be sure they said the same thing. Besides, if she went alone, they might think she was just making it all up, that she was hysterical. She probably looked crazy from being mad at Ash and running through the woods.

Lexi sent 'k' back and turned in the opposite direction of the station, toward home. If Monica didn't come right away, she'd get her mom to take her. One way or another, she would tell her story before the night ended.

Just to be careful, she turned her attention to the street, scanning in both directions as she walked, listening for the rumble of Ash's car. There was no familiar engine sound or flash of red in traffic. A while later, wiped out from the whole ordeal, she trudged toward her front steps. The spot where Dale's truck usually sat was empty. Would her mother be rumpled on the couch, sobbing because they'd had another fight? If that was the case, she'd better wait for Monica outside. Maybe she wouldn't even go in to let her mom know she was home from being out with Ash. No point in adding yet another useless emotional scene to the night.

Lexi stepped softly across the grass, her gaze fixed on the glaring porch light illuminating the front of the house. For once she didn't care that her neighborhood was kind of shabby, that her house was plain and small. She could sit in one of the chairs, catch her breath, and be safe and alone for a few minutes. Some time to get her head together was exactly what she needed before dealing with Monica and the cops. But before she reached the first step up to the porch, a sudden jerk from behind stopped her in her tracks. It only took a split second for her to realize someone was holding on to her. In that tiny fraction of time, the adrenaline, still fresh in her body from what happened at the lake, flared and her body charged with energy.

Her first instinct, to thrust the attacker away while dashing for her door, ended up being the worst thing she could've done. Because the stranger grabbed her wrists and wrenched them up, twisting her arms. She thrashed, jerking side to side, throwing her weight against the force holding her, but the actions did no good. A savage scream gathered in her throat, but before she could free it from her lungs a sweet, moist rag filled her mouth.

Still struggling, Lexi made her second mistake—she gasped for air. The noxious fumes of the rag flooded her mind, and her world went black.

Chapter Fourteen

What Fun Doesn't Look Like

Stinging pains like a million tiny needles jabbed into Lexi's hands, wrists and arms. The fiery sensation burned deep inside her, numbing her muscles and making her feel only half there, like someone had pulled off her arms and legs then tossed her down, leaving her to wriggle across the floor like a worm. That couldn't be, she told herself.

Wake up.

Wake up now and fight.

Her stomach turned, clenching as a horrific odor oozed into her pores and swelled her lungs. With each breath, she pulled in more of horrible smell until the stench permeated her body. Gradually she came to, working to open her eyes and struggling to remember.

So relieved to see her own front porch light.

Almost reaching her front door, a brief struggle…

The gray rag, smothering her…

That wicked smell, the blackness…

What had she noticed, right before being grabbed?

Step by step, she flipped back through her memory, narrowing her attention to that single fine line of events until she hit on the one thing that had stood out to her at the moment. The vacant spot in her driveway usually filled with her stepdad's van. A rush of disgust rolled through her. Dale Welks had sunk to a new low, kidnapping his own stepdaughter. The possibility stirred the queasiness in her stomach, made her aching arms and hands throb with new fierceness.

No. She couldn't let herself freak out. That was the last thing she needed, wild fear and anger wiping out her ability to think.

Lexi returned to her thinking. The memories started to fill in, especially the pieces of the park — her starting to think Monica was right, racing away from Ash. The fury in his voice, the hint of a threat. Was he so spiteful that he'd take her? His tone had softened after she'd run away. His calls had become less hostile, more pleading. Did that mean something?

Wiggling against the throbbing in her limbs, she tried to get the feeling to return so she could use her muscles. The tingling in her arms and legs was brutal but she continued on, anxious to get through the pain and move. Lexi struggled to sit and loosen her bound wrists, but when she moved her fingers she realized her hands were covered with a plastic bag. Even though another surge of fear threatened to make her lose control, she continued bending her fingers up and down over and over until the ripples of pain softened enough that she had sensation in the tips of her fingers.

The inside of the bag was damp. Sticky, maybe. From her own sweat? The plastic was pretty thin, grocery store shopping bag most likely. She wiggled, trying to poke holes in the plastic and fighting the twine wrapped around her wrists. With each movement, the stench surrounding her flowed deeper into her skin, saturating each quivering inch of her inside and out.

"Lexi?"

She stiffened.

Was the sound real? Or was that stink making her lose her mind?

She held her breath, kept herself completely still.

The voice came again. "You okay?"

She tensed, braced to defend herself as best she could.

"Lexi, it's me, Monica. Are you okay?"

She sucked in air and ended up gagging on the swollen stink of the dark place. Blinking into the thick black air, Lexi forced her eyes to adjust. About ten feet away, the silhouette of Monica's dark hair formed.

"Lexi? You okay?" The rustle of plastic being twisted came through the darkness. "He got me too."

"Monica?" Disbelief swelled in Lexi's mind. She fought against the confusion, trying to clear her thoughts.

"Yeah. It's me." The crinkle of plastic came again. "He got me too. I'm tied up, just like you."

That made no sense.

"What does he want with you?" she asked, even though she was still uncertain about who had taken her. Taken *them*? "What does he want with me?"

"I don't know."

They'd said Monica had gone missing hours before she'd gone out with Ash. How long had she been gone before anyone noticed? Terror climbed up her back and cut off her air as more questions surfaced, bobbing along with the others. How long had she been out? Where the hell were they? She tried to speak, but her throat had tightened and the only sound that came out was a hiss. The hiss turned into a cough, which turned into a gag. Soon Lexi was fighting for control of her breathing. She let the shudders in her lungs roll through her until finally the heaving stopped and she was left with a manageable pant. Inhaling through her mouth made the stench less unbearable so she continued, pulling the air through her mouth then exhaling through her nose.

The rasp of Monica's sharp breath crept through the bleak stench. "We're in trouble."

Lexi continued focusing on her breathing, doing what she had to to straighten out her mind. That meant she had to stop thinking about what made sense and what did not. Speculation would make her head spin and get her nowhere. She needed to concentrate on the facts.

One new fact bubbled up — she had no real proof that Monica was actually tied up. The girl could easily be pretending. Of all this things she'd considered, that one, given everything that had happened, made the most sense.

"You!" Lexi wriggled from side to side, anxious now to get the feeling back in her legs so she could get to her feet. The other girl's guilty silence exploded between them. She used her anger to energize herself and give herself the will to fight harder. "What kind of freak are you?"

"It's not me," Monica replied, her voice urgent. "Don't you get it? We're in trouble. Real trouble."

Lexi had fallen for the girl's lies before. That was in the past. "Who helped you?" She thrashed more, biting at the plastic covering her hands, jerking at the twine to free her wrists.

"Lexi!" Monica insisted, her voice taking on an unfamiliar edge. "I didn't have anything to do with this. As a matter of fact, if I hadn't come to your house, trying to help you, I wouldn't be here."

Trying to help her? The absurd comment stopped her cold. "You didn't come to my house. And what do you mean *trying to help* me?" Lexi spat in disgust, the stiff cord cutting into her ankles as she squirmed against the cold, hard floor beneath her. "Like I'm supposed to believe that."

"It's the truth. I didn't want you to have to go to the police station alone. Remember?"

There was a shuffling sound. Lexi's eyes had adjusted enough that she could tell it was from Monica. Pebbles ground against the cement floor as she scooted over, the movement slow because the other girl was tied up too.

Lexi fought for another breath, gagging as the stench filled her stomach with bile and made her head swim. The smell was foul, unnatural, unimaginable in its awfulness. This time she ignored the fear that came each time she pulled the nastiness of it into her body, scrambling despite the agony until her legs came under her. Leaning against the rough wall, she fought the binds and the pain until she was upright. Her legs were bound so balance was difficult, she swayed awkwardly then hopped to keep from toppling over.

But it was no good, the movement made the panting return, only this time she forgot to breathe in through her mouth. Suddenly she couldn't stop heaving. Her lungs twisted and her knees started to shake. The precious little control she'd managed to gather started to slip away, bit by bit.

"Lexi. Lexi!" Monica worked herself over a few more inches, until they were close enough to brush shoulders. "You're going to make yourself pass out. Sit back down. You need to put your head between your legs and breathe slowly. In and then out."

"No, I-I have — I — have — " Lexi hopped forward but her knees buckled — she went down in a heap.

"It's okay. We're going to be okay," Monica whispered, gradually scooting to where Lexi had fallen.

Lexi's check stung where it had hit the floor and the pain radiated down her neck, blending in with the pain in her arms and back. She squeezed her eyes shut, trying to hold back the flood of hot tears as the waves of queasiness and the vise-like grip of panic tightened around her chest.

"Look at me," Monica pleaded, leaning her shoulder into her

Lexi squeezed her eyelids tighter, shook her head. The reality was too much. Excruciating. Absolutely unbearable.

"Please?" the other girl asked again. "Open your eyes. It's just the two of us here. We have to work together. We've got to keep things from getting worse."

But Lexi couldn't open her eyes, and she couldn't stop smelling the horrible smell, the sickly sweet scent that coated her body, filled her head and soaked her through and through. She tried breathing through her mouth again but now that she'd taken in so much of the smell, the heavy, full rush of air only made the repulsion worse. Her stomach convulsed and her lungs trembled. Her last thought before blacking out was the memory of Ash on the park bench, trying to smother her with the blanket.

* * * *

Consciousness came back to Lexi, brought on by the sounds of heavy footsteps and loud breathing. She opened her eyes and saw a person coming toward her, a bright, swinging camp-style lantern out in front of a tall, wide-shouldered body. Yellow light cut up from beneath the guy's chin, distorting a battered catcher's mask, hiding his face and muffling his voice.

"Hi." The fingers of his left hand twitched. "Having fun? I hope so, because I know having fun is all you really care about."

He leaned down, the huge mask swallowing his face.

Lexi's skin burned hot, her muscles flicked. Was this part of a dream? Something she was remembering from before she'd been snatched? No, she realized when he spoke again. This was now.

"How are my special video sweethearts? Enjoying each other?" The lantern swung high, squeaking as it swayed on its handle. The light danced across the floor and the guy in the mask twisted, adding, "And our guest, of course. You're enjoying him as well. Am I right?"

Lexi's gaze followed the path of the light. Her gaze moved along, following the filmy, lemon-yellow path. The illumination stopped and she saw what the guy intended for her to see.

No, not what.

But who.

Jon Eagle.

He was seated on a wooden crate and tied to a pillar, ropes and brightly colored coils wrapped around, cutting into his decaying flesh. His clothes hung limply, looking like clothes that had been stretched across and around him after he'd died then started to rot. Empty plastic ice bags covered his twisted feet and filled his lap. Some of the bags had blue penguins, some had a cluster of red snowflakes. Empty two-liter bottles of Coke circled his feet. Two shrunken eyes, floating above hollowed cheeks, stared straight ahead. An open mouth screamed silently.

The shriek that gathered inside Lexi came out as a garbled, defeated wail. The pitiful sound of her own cry made her shiver then tremble with an odd intensity. The vibrations in her body were a feral combination of terror and brute force. She let out another wail, hoping that the wild strength in her would win out.

The person with the lantern rushed forward, shouting over her shrieks. "Stop screaming."

Lexi kept on, hoping that she'd find some mystical power to escape or that someone would hear her, or that she would wake up. She stared ahead, watching the gentle swaying of the lantern and its spilled light as she howled. On and on she went, battling with herself to keep from giving in to the helplessness of her situation.

The guy set the lantern down and pulled a rag from his pocket. Even though she knew what was coming, she didn't stop screaming. The sound was all she had, the only way to fight back, and so she used it. He held the lantern up, taunting her. From beside her, she heard Monica urging her to stop with the noise but she had no intention of listening.

He took one step forward.

Then another.

And one more.

In a long, smooth, motion, so graceful it looked like he did it all the time, he swooped in and stuffed the nasty thing into her hollering mouth. She recognized the scent and, realizing that she had to fight another way, twisted, willing herself to stay conscious.

Don't let him win.

Be strong.

But whatever was on the rag found its way into her lungs and wiped her out, the last of her screams fading into the desolation of her mind.

Chapter Fifteen

Girls Nite Out

Lexi fought the fogginess in her mind and finally won. With her next breath the sweet stench filled her head and it all came back. Every little detail. She opened her eyes and came face to face with the liar. "You said he was alive, Monica. You said you got texts from him!"

"Stop screaming, Lexi." After a few seconds of silence, Monica's voice came through the darkness. "I only said that to keep you from going to the cops."

They should have gone to the cops right away. The very next morning, when they'd realized what had happened and that people were starting to wonder where he was and what had happened to him. Lexi sagged. If only she could go back and do that over. Do it all over. Not just that morning, or the night before, but the whole summer. Months of idiocy and ugliness. All of the worst things she'd ever done, all within one summer break.

"That was stupid. If you didn't want to go to the cops, that would've been fine. You should have told me the truth and let me go. I could have taken all the blame."

"I know that now. But I thought it was Ash, not Zeke."

The image of the catcher's mask rose up in Lexi's mind. "It's too late now, Monica. It's too late to do the right thing." She fought the fresh coil of hysteria spiraling through her as she added, "And it's too late for us."

Monica lowered her voice. "No, it's not too late for us. We're going to get out of this. If you'll just stop screaming the next time Zeke comes in."

More insanity. More random pieces she couldn't fit together. "What's Zeke got against Jon? Or me?"

"Stop asking questions and help me figure a way out of this." She was jerking her legs back and forth, using the heels of her boots to try to snag the twine.

Lexi couldn't let the questions go. "I didn't have anything to do with posting that video."

Monica sighed. "Girls showing off their boobs is no big deal. Especially when they knew exactly what they were doing."

Lexi followed Monica's motions and started working at the twine around her ankles too. "I guess that's true. Sort of." She stopped moving her legs and lifted her arms. "But that doesn't explain this."

Monica didn't even look over when she replied. "He did more than that. He made ones in the bathroom too."

"What are you talking about?"

The twine around Monica's legs suddenly came free, and she kicked it away. It flew up and landed beside

Lexi. "He made videos of girls going pee. In the bathroom."

That couldn't be true. "How do you know?"

"He showed me."

Monica's response sent chills down Lexi's arms. "You're both sick." Seeing Monica's legs free gave her the encouragement she needed. She kept struggling.

"I'm not sick. He is. That's why I uploaded that one video, to get him into trouble and stop him."

Something about that didn't ring true but her binds were almost off. "What about Jon?" The pressure from the twine gave way and her legs were free.

"I don't know." Monica's voice softened. "Probably knew him from baseball or some other place. Whatever happened with him and Jon has nothing to do with us."

"Look at that." Lexi tipped her head toward Jon's body, hearing her voice rise but unable to stop herself from screaming. Her next words came out in a low shriek. "He's dead, Monica. And in here. So, yeah, it does have something to do with us."

"I know," Monica said, her voice level. "But we have to think right now. Not freak out."

That was true. And looking at Jon's body, now that she wasn't terrified and hysterical, made her realize she had to act. Not scream or panic. The longer they took, the more chance there was that Zeke would come back. Lexi twisted against the ropes securing her wrists. "We have to find a way out of here. Where's the door? Did you try to find it while I was passed out?"

"I was out of it too. He kept rubbing that rag in my face, popping in and out, threatening me with more. Then you got here, and, well, I didn't want to leave you."

"This is—we—" Giving up on her wrists for the moment, Lexi scrambled to her feet. "Stand up. We have to get out of here. Now. Before he comes back."

The rough cement wall tore Lexi's delicate blue sweater, ripping it to shreds, but soon she was on her feet with Monica beside her. Blood flowed in her legs, fiery pins and needles burning her thighs and calves. Ignoring the pain, she scooted sideways, sliding her plastic-coated hands along the wall. Her feet were still partially numb and she moved carefully, doing everything she could to not trip. She moved past wooden crates, trash and invisible creatures scurrying along the walls. Her foot slid on a slippery plastic bag.

Monica gagged.

The stench got more intense as they moved. Lexi concentrated on not getting sick, telling herself to think about anything except what she was dealing with. A few steps later, she was surprised to find herself thinking about her mom and how badly she wanted to get home.

Monica was right. For now, they had to work together. She'd worry about later, later. "You there?" she asked.

"Yeah, I'm with you." The other girl coughed, then said, "I'm fine. Keep going."

The room seemed long. The floor was scattered with weird-looking beige foam shapes, broken sticks and empty glass bottles. Three small barred windows let in smudgy rays of light.

Monica said what Lexi was thinking as they passed under the openings. "Even if we did break the glass, getting past the bars would be impossible."

That was obvious. "Look for the door."

As they crept past Jon's rotting body, Lexi tried not to look at what was left of his face. But it was nearly impossible to avert her gaze from the corpse being caressed by the misty rays of light fighting through the grimy windows. The worst part was his filmy eyes, staring blindly forward, as though he was waiting. She tried not to think about that night, and how he'd been goofy and happy, wanting to impress them with facts about his expensive racing bike.

"Lexi." Monica spoke weakly from behind. "I-I think I'm going to puke."

"Go ahead if you have to, just keep moving."

Lexi skidded on something. A pile of red second-place ribbons, each with scientific symbols in the center. Then it hit her, the answer to a question she should've been asking. "This is the science club building. You know that, right?"

"Um, yeah. You're right. I mean, yeah, I know." Monica's voice got lighter. "It is. Close to home, just have to get out of here."

"You guys had your meetings here, right? So you must know your way around."

"Oh, sure. I do. Go around the corner, the door's that way. Look for the stairs."

They made their way around the corner, inching along. The farther they moved from the windows, the dimmer it became. Without the shadows from the street lamps, they had to stay close to the wall to avoid running into boxes on the floor or the occasional piece of broken glass. Soon they were standing in near-blackness. Keeping her left foot steady, Lexi circled her right one, hoping to bump into the stairs. Her toe connected with a cracked wooden slat — the outline of steps. "This way."

Stumbling as she searched for each step with her toe, she climbed until a cold, hard metal lattice scraped below her foot. She'd reached the top of some sort of platform.

She moved forward, then stopped to check on Monica. "You there?"

"Right behind you," Monica replied, her voice growing stronger.

Lexi moved along until a scuttling sound stopped her in her tracks. She waited, trying to listen over the thumping of her heart and the murmur of Monica's breathing. "That you?"

The other girl bumped into her. "What?"

"That noise," she whispered.

"No. It's not me."

Lexi strained, holding her entire body still. "Maybe it's a rat or something."

The swish came again.

The second time rougher, closer.

Louder.

It wasn't a mouse or rat. It wasn't any creature.

The hinges of the door squeaked and a beam of light pierced Lexi's gaze. She reached back and leaned against Monica.

"Hey! Hello?"

Lexi's muscles flashed hot. She tensed, unsure of whether to rush forward or flee back the way they'd come.

The voice came again, louder. "Who's in here?"

Her mind had to be playing tricks. "Ash?"

"Lexi?"

She dove into the darkness, flailing her bag-coated hands and tumbling until she fell into Ash's arms.

Monica was right behind her, trying to grab them both with her bound hands until the three of them fell against the wall, sliding down until they hit the metal steps.

Monica smacked at Ash. "What are you doing here, Ash?"

"I was going to the weight room, trying to blow off some steam from — you know." He glanced at Lexi, his eyes filled with apology. "Anyway, I heard the screaming, so I — " His lips curled as his lifted his head, trying to look through the darkness. "What is — What's going on?"

After a beat of silence, she felt him gagging, so she leaned back to give him room to breathe. "Breathe through your mouth then out through your nose," she said.

"What's that smell?" he asked, his chest still heaving.

Monica scrambled to her feet. "It's Jon — "

"Zeke killed him and took us." Lexi grabbed at Ash, trying with her covered hands to pull him up through the darkness as she said, "We have to get out of here before he comes back. Hurry, stand up. Let's go."

"What the hell are you talking about?" Ash got up, weaving, probably from the stench. "I just saw Zeke."

Lexi shoved her plastic-wrapped hands in Ash's face, rubbing them together to make a rustling sound. "He tied us up. He killed Jon, Ash. That's what that smell is."

"Over there."

Holding his hands over his mouth, Ash searched out into the room, his gaze circling until finally stopping on the outline of Jon Eagle's body, visible beneath the thin light coming through the window. He took a slow step forward, then another, then leaped the last three, covering the last few yards in seconds.

Lexi rushed after him then stopped to watch him gradually reach out. His hand hovered in the pale rays of light coming through the window, his fingers wavering as he reached forward. Her stomach knotted as she watched him touch the dead, rotting corpse that had once been his best friend.

He spoke. "Jon. What happened? It's really over now." The last word came out as a sob, the sounds of his voice tapering off to a wordless jumble.

Monica and Lexi reached him at the same time. "We have to go, come on — "

"Monica's right, Ash. We have to get out of here before Zeke comes back." She pushed him away from Jon's body, toward the door. "It'll be okay. We just have to leave. Now."

Chapter Sixteen

Right Back Where We Started

Lexi looked at the outline of the old science club building and pulled in gulps of fresh air. The action helped clear her lungs and ease some of the tension in her muscles, but nothing could get rid of the vision of Jon's rotting body, tied to a post and covered with plastic bags. They had to get the hell out of there.

With quick small bites, Monica used her teeth to tear through the bag covering her own hands then tore at the one wrapped around Lexi's. Jabbing Ash with her elbow, she said, "Come on, Ash, help me get her untied."

But Ash didn't move. He stared at the door, still hanging open on its rusty hinges. His face was flat and pale, and his mouth hung open. As soon as the bag was gone and the binding was exposed, Monica took care of the knots, then Lexi undid hers. The pieces of twine fell to the ground, landing on top of the brittle leaves.

Hands finally free, Lexi pushed Ash to his Mustang, parked way past the single streetlight that had sent the pale rays in through the windows. Obviously he wasn't much use in his present condition. They didn't have time for him to snap out of it. "Ash, give me your keys. We're going to the police station. Now. We have to go right now."

He stumbled along, still looking over his shoulder at the door to the building as they hurried away from it. "We shouldn't leave Jon in there," he murmured as he started to drag his feet.

"Ash," she said again, this time more sharply. "Give me your keys. That's what Jon would want, for us to go get the police and tell them about Zeke."

Finally he turned his head forward. He dug the keys out, then handed them over to Lexi, who hit the fob to unlock the doors. Monica stuffed Ash into the back seat, then got into the passenger seat, and Lexi got behind the wheel.

The engine rumbled to life. The warehouse disappeared in the rearview mirror as Lexi hit the gas. She wasn't nearly as good as Ash with the standard transmission, but thankfully Cherry Grove's over-the-top school system insisted that their driver's ed program included manual transmission lessons.

Monica braced herself as Lexi blew through a stop sign and took a sharp turn. The car bucked some as she shifted, but she managed to keep it going forward without stalling.

"Ash?" Monica lifted herself up so she could look over the seat at Ash. "How did Zeke even know that place was there? Did you tell him?"

"Obviously Zeke's been planning this for a while," he said, his voice thin.

Lexi sucked in a deep breath, steadying her hand on the steering wheel as she raced the Mustang closer to the police station. Houses flashed past. She blew another stop sign, downshifted roughly to take the corner.

"Lexi? Are you sure you should go to the police?" Ash asked.

Lexi glanced into the rearview mirror. His face looked wrong and he was slumped down. What had happened to that forceful, furious guy of a couple hours ago? Yes, the scene in the science building had been a shock, but shouldn't he be angry about that too? His reaction to his friend being dead didn't make sense. He was useless right now. It was up to her to make the decisions. "Of course we have to go to the cops."

"That's right, Ash," Monica said, her voice strong. She spun around and dropped back into the passenger seat. "Zeke is still out there—who knows what he might do next?"

"But, because of, well…" Ash started drumming his fingers across the top of the seat, his fingertips brushing Lexi's hair. "The cops might think you did it. Killed Jon, I mean."

It took a second for Lexi to get that he was talking to her. "Why the hell would they think that?"

He spoke again, his voice still flat but louder and stronger. "Because of Peter, like, maybe you actually did that, and everybody knows you hate Monica."

"I don't hate Monica, and Peter—is—was…" Lexi glanced over, trying to see Ash's face, but it was in shadows. "Didn't you say you just saw Zeke?"

"Yeah." He kept staring ahead, drumming his fingers, flipping the ends of her hair. "At your house."

Her stomach clenched as the doused fire of adrenaline flared again. This time it blazed quickly, flaring through her body, igniting each nerve ending.

Think, she reminded herself.

Think.

Not react.

She looked at Ash in the rearview window. "Why would Zeke go to my house?"

"He had to drop off some equipment, same as me, for your stepdad. I wanted to see you, you know, to say sorry for being an ass at the park. I know I haven't said much about Peter and Jon, but I've been so stressed about them. I think I said some stuff I shouldn't have."

His need to apologize meant nothing, but the thought of Zeke at her house filled her with terror and rage. Monica had posted the video to Facebook, not her. If Zeke hurt her mom, there was no telling what Lexi would do.

Monica twisted back around, then held out her hand, palm up. "Ash, give me your cell."

He patted himself and shook his head. "I guess I lost it."

The rebuilt engine roared as Lexi hit the gas harder.

"Seriously, Ash?" Monica flipped back around to dig through the jumble of maps and papers tucked in the narrow glove compartment. "Not in here." She snapped the tiny door shut, glaring over the top of the seat. "Just like always. Do you really have to screw everything up? Every single thing, every single time?"

Lexi spun around a corner. She was ready to ask Monica what she was talking about, but the other girl was still raging and besides, they were almost at her street.

"You and Zeke both. Damn." She fell into the back seat, grumbling to herself. "What total losers."

Finally, they reached her house. Lexi stomped on the brakes, making the tires squeal. She parked Ash's car, climbed out, then ran to throw open her front door.

She ran in.

Empty.

Lexi caught a glimpse of Monica rushing in behind her as she raced up the stairs, shouting for her mom as she went up two steps at a time. She checked every room. *Empty.*

Downstairs, Monica shouted too, but no replies came.

Lexi jogged down the steps, went straight to the wall phone, dialed her mom's cell. It rang several times then went to voicemail.

Time for the last resort.

Dale.

She dialed. He answered on the third ring.

"Is my mom with you?" she asked, hoping her voice sounded calm. Or at least not as hysterical as she felt.

"What kind of trouble are you in this time?"

Not now. "Please, Dale, this is important. Is my mom with you?"

"Where are you?"

Lexi gritted her teeth, then forced out a reply. "I'm at home, looking for my mom. Do you know where she is?"

He ignored her question. "Ash stopped by to ask about the equipment, told me you ditched him. I don't know what kind of games you're playing, using that kid —"

While he was going on, a noise like a child's laugh came from the background. He wasn't alone. After the sound ended, he came back on the line. "After Ash left, your mom lost it, insisting we go look for you to make sure you were safe. I told her I'd finally had enough of your crap. I have better things to do than drive around looking for your sorry ass."

Monica started pulling on Lexi's arm, but she ignored the sharp tugs, focusing instead on trying to get what she needed from Dale. "She's out looking for me?"

"I guess." There was a pause, then more of the high-pitched chatter. Once again, he waited for the sound to stop before speaking to her. "I gotta go."

He disconnected.

Lexi let out a breath as she looked at Monica. "She's out driving around, looking for me. What? Why are you—?"

"I found your bag on the ground next to the sidewalk. He must've tossed it there."

Lexi grabbed it and dug out her phone. A row of texts and missed calls from her mom.

Monica grabbed Lexi and pulled her toward the front door. "We should go look for your mom. We gotta go find her."

Lexi stalled, her heart pounding. "We have to call the cops."

"Give me your phone, I'll call them on the way. You look out the window for your mom."

Jogging to the car, Lexi handed her phone to Monica. Monica took it, swung open Ash's car door and pointed to the back seat. Lexi dove in and seconds later they were racing away from her house, Ash behind the wheel, finally looking alert.

Holding Lexi's phone, Monica asked, "Did Dale mention Zeke? Say whether he stopped by or not?"

"I'll go down Grove, toward school," Ash said when he reached the end of her street.

The thought of going anywhere near the school made Lexi sick, but it did make sense that her mom would look for her there. "Okay, but check by the park too."

Instead of responding to her, Ash looked at Monica. "What do you think, Monica?"

Monica held Lexi's phone on her knee and twisted back and repeated her question. "Did your— Did Dale say anything about Zeke coming to your house?"

"No, he didn't mention Zeke. He said Ash came by to ask about the, the—" Ash made a sharp turn, throwing Lexi across the tiny back seat. She reached out to brace herself, her hand landing on a rough canvas bag. She pushed the bag—a bat slid out, then a catcher's mask tumbled over it and rolled to a stop by her feet.

She kicked it away. "Ash? Where's Zeke?"

Ash stared straight ahead, the school coming into view ahead. "How the hell should I know?"

"Monica, give me my phone. I want to call the cops. Now."

"No. You watch for your mom, I'll call." Monica slowly starting tapping on the screen.

"Ash killed Jon," Lexi said, realizing that maybe she should have kept the words to herself.

"No, I didn't." He shot a glance at Monica, a flicker of pain going across his face. "I'm keeping Jon. He's not leaving, he's my best friend."

Lexi grabbed the mask and held it up. "You're crazy, Ash."

Monica twisted to see what was in Lexi's hand.

Ash shot around another corner and hit the gas. Lexi held on to the seat as his Mustang rumbled past Cherry Grove High. Headlights flashed in the rearview mirror, and he hit the gas to put distance between him and the car behind them.

Monica lifted her palms. "What the hell are you going to do? Just drive away from what you've done?"

"Shut up, Monica. I'm done listening to you."

"You should just turn yourself in," she said, turning to look out of the window. "That way the cops will be easier on you."

Monica was pretending to be calm and Lexi, trying to follow her example, willed herself to think clearly. The car rumbled farther away from the school, in the opposite direction from the park.

Lexi knew this stretch well. There wasn't anything or anyone for a couple of miles. Overgrown fields of gnarled trees and closed-up cherry processing plants. There was no telling where Ash might take them or what he could do to them once he got them there. A guy who was capable of tying up his best friend and watching him rot was capable of anything.

Monica stared straight ahead, her hands gripping the door handle. Lexi wedged herself between the seats and readied her hands at her sides.

Ash continued to mutter to himself about plans and cops and friends.

Lexi steadied herself and waited.

The last of the abandoned cherry tree fields zipped past. The first of the familiar overgrown weeds and shrubs that hid the old Westerville baseball diamond came into view.

Lexi lunged, grabbing the steering wheel and jerking it to the left. Ash fought back, lifting his elbows and throwing his head back as the car left the road, spun across the gravel shoulder and hit the ditch with a sharp jolt.

Monica shrieked. The engine wailed.

The struggle worked to Lexi's advantage. He took his hands off the wheel. She grabbed it, jerked again and the car swerved, hitting the row of shrubs full force.

The car shook as it bounced over the rutted ground until finally slamming into the long-forgotten backstop. Ash threw open the door and rolled out. Monica spilled out from the other side. Lexi scrambled after them.

Monica headed straight for Ash. "Stop running, Ash. It's over."

"Stop her, Lexi," Ash yelled, swiping at tears. "You're the only one who knows how to control her. You have to stop her, otherwise—"

Monica shoved him from behind and the two of them tumbled backward over the batters' bench.

Lexi dove into the tangle of arms and legs. The darkness and tall grass made it impossible to see, so she had to go by touch to figure out who was who. Twisting and turning, Lexi fought to peel Ash off Monica.

Above them someone shouted, "Get off my daughter."

Her mom, with her hands gripped tightly around a baseball bat, looking frazzled but surer of herself than Lexi had seen in a long time.

Ash scrambled away and got to his feet. He held his hands up. "Wait, Mrs. Welks. Everything's okay here. I can explain."

"You know what?" She raised the bat, twisted her waist. "I've had it with liars." With that, she swung low, hitting him right behind the knees.

He went down with a howl and a heavy thump.

Lexi's mom hovered over him. "Get up again and next time I'm aiming for your head."

Monica held up Lexi's phone. "It's time to call the cops."

Chapter Seventeen

Then Again, Maybe It Does Matter How You Play the Game

"You sure you're ready for this?" Lexi's mom asked as they neared the front of Cherry Grove High.

"Sure, no problem." Maybe when the nightmare was really over she'd take a few days off, but not yet.

Lexi's mom rolled past the drop-off curb and pulled into a spot. "I didn't mean school, I meant the appointment with Mrs. Howell."

"Oh, sure. She's cool. You'll like her."

Lexi reached for the door but her mom stopped her by putting a hand on her arm.

"It's not too late, is it? For us?"

"What made you change your mind? About Dale?"

"When Ash showed up, saying you'd ditched him, Dale and I argued about going to look for you. He kept refusing to go, saying I was being overprotective and a fool for thinking you'd obey the curfew. He kept saying we should let Ash go find you. That's when it was obvious that Dale cared more about what Ash — his star pitcher — thought, than whether or not you were safe.

"While I was driving around, scared out of my mind looking for you, you know where I found Dale?"

Lexi shrugged.

"At that diner. In the back room. With some twenty-year-old waitress."

"Sick."

"That's one way of putting it."

Her mom pulled the keys out of the ignition and dropped them into her purse. "I should've accepted what you said, that something was wrong."

"All I wanted was for it to be just the two of us, you know, like this — just talking, doing stuff, depending on each other — like before."

The image of her mom taking down Ash with one swing of the bat snapped into her head. "Actually, I do have Dale to thank for my rescue."

Her mom sagged against the window. "Dale? Hello, I'm the one who showed up."

"I know, but you never would've found me if super-suspicious Dale hadn't put that tracker on my phone."

Lexi pointed to her bag. "I wouldn't care if you kept it. That way you could come and save me again."

"It's gone already. Just like Dale." She swung the door open. Lexi followed.

The scene in front of the school was the usual — clear sun glinting off the factory-fresh gloss of new Acuras, Volvos and a couple of plain Fords. Pieces of Lady Gaga, Cake and, thanks to Spaz, ICP swam through the air. Clusters of freshman girls lingered by the doors, each girl tapping on her phone, talking and checking out the older guys.

Jazz slipped through girls, rushed toward Lexi and threw her arms around her. "You have to tell me everything."

Lexi hugged her back, laughing when Jazz wouldn't let go of her. "I will. I promise."

"You're sitting with me, right?"

Jazz pointed to a banner Lexi had somehow missed. The words 'Fresh Start Pep Rally!' screamed at her in bright red letters. The black outline on the banner made it look hideous.

Jazz finally let go of Lexi. "This school is ridiculous, I know, but at least we don't have to go to class."

"Of course I'm sitting with you, but I'm going to be a bit late. Mom and I are going to see Mrs. Howell."

"Oh, hey, Ms. Welks."

"Hi, Jasmine." Lexi's mom gave Jazz a quick hug. "I'm glad your parents let you come back. Lexi's been missing you."

After Lexi promised to find Jazz at the pep rally, they split up. Once Jazz was out of earshot, Lexi stepped away from her mom. "I'll meet you at the office. I have to get some stuff from my locker."

* * * *

The girl's bathroom was empty.

Lexi went to stand by the mirror then sent a quick text to Zeke —

Now.

She pulled out her lip gloss, opened it and waited.

"So what is it that's so epically urgent?" Monica asked as she rushed in.

Lexi leaned against the bathroom wall, positioning herself in the corner just the way she and Zeke had set it up. "Did you hear they found Jon's bike glove in Ash's bedroom?"

"So what? Aren't you glad I kept you from going to the cops?"

"No, actually I'm not. You told me Jon was okay."

"That was to keep you quiet. And you can see I was right about Ash. I put the glove in his room just to make sure he didn't get away with anything."

"He could've killed us."

Monica's laugh came out as a hoarse bark. "He wasn't going to kill us. And it's all over now. Be glad nobody ever figured out that Jon was with us that night. Drunk Jon was our little present to poor sad Ash."

A shiver ran down Lexi's back, but she hid it by putting on another coat of lip gloss. "Not our present. Your present. I don't remember any of that."

"Yeah, you never did get a handle on the drinking." Monica looked her up and down. "But it was fun sharing our little secrets, wasn't it?"

Even if the cops charged her for her involvement, Lexi had to keep talking to get everything she needed. "Guess seeing a dead guy doesn't freak you out like it does me."

"That was always the problem with everyone in science club. So squeamish, always acting like babies when it was time to do something real."

A roar of applause from the start of the assembly was followed by the stomping of hundreds of feet. Lexi waited until it faded. "I'm not squeamish. I'm not afraid to do something real."

"Yeah. Sure, Lexi." Monica straightened and turned sideways, admiring her perfect boobs. "You keep thinking that and maybe I'll let you be second place boosters' president. You know, like a runner-up? You could be my personal ass, not just one day but every day. What do you think about that?"

"I think I'll do something real, just to show you I can."

Monica paused, stopping to give her a more serious once-over. "You'd be surprised how exciting it is, doing something just to prove to yourself you can. And it's such a rush when it works out."

Monica started to leave, but Lexi grabbed her arm.

"What do you think will happen to Ash?"

"Who the hell cares?"

Lexi squeezed her fingers around Monica's wrist. "Ash tried to frame Z."

"If he'd been able to hold himself together, it would've worked. He always did crack at the worst possible time." Monica smirked so hard it was a snarl. "Guess that's why he was never his dad's favorite." She yanked her arm free and left.

* * * *

"I saved a copy on my hard drive. Here's yours." Zeke held out a tiny flash drive. "Best video you ever made."

Lexi took the drive. "Thanks."

"Glad to do it."

"Sorry about what happened to you. That crap Monica pulled was nasty."

He shrugged. "Thanks for believing me about not making those other ones, in the bathroom." He grinned and Lexi saw a flash of that side of Z that had caught her attention before everything went to hell. "I should've seen it coming," he said.

"I bet Ash feels the same way."

"He didn't kill Jon, you know," he said.

Lexi let out a slow breath. "Or Peter. I haven't quite figured how she did it, but I know she did both of them."

"That's pretty extreme, just to shut me up about the video."

Tracing the edge of the drive with her fingernail, she added, "And to prove she could do it."

"That's epically wrong."

He was right, of course, that it was wrong to do something that twisted just to prove you could get away with it. But Lexi was starting to see what Monica meant about doing something real. Guess the trick was to define 'real' the right way.

"Putting this out there might screw you up, too."

"I know. But I'm done with secrets and lies."

Zeke pointed to the flash drive. "They won't be able to use that in court."

"I know." Lexi dropped the flash drive into her bag. "It's a start, though, and sooner or later the cops will figure it all out, then that girl will finally get what's coming."

About the Author

Isabelle Drake got her start writing confession stories for pulp magazines like *True Confessions* and *True Love*. Since publishing those first few stories she has written in many genres, but tends to write about everyday people in extraordinary situations.

When away from her keyboard, she likes watching classic horror films, especially Hammer films such as the *Karnstein Trilogy*, and reading (of course). An avid traveler, she'll go just about anywhere—at least once—to meet people and get story ideas.

Isabelle loves to hear from readers. You can find her contact information, website details and author profile page at http://www.finch-books.com.